Print Edition ISBN: 978-1-7330721-4-4

Cover Designed by Hang Le
Cover Model Jordan Steele
Photographer Chris Davis at Specular
Edited by Editing 4 Indies and Personal Touch Editing

❀ Created with Vellum

Books by Jill Ramsower

The Five Families Series
Forever Lies
Never Truth
Blood Always
Where Loyalties Lie
Impossible Odds
Absolute Silence
Perfect Enemies

The Savage Pride Duet
Savage Pride
Silent Prejudice

Of Myth and Man Series
Curse & Craving
Venom & Vice
Blood & Breath
Siege & Seduction

NEVER TRUTH

JILL RAMSOWER

CHAPTER 1
Sofia

THEN

"Please, Daddy, can I go with you? I don't wanna go with Mama. I want to go with you and Marco to the movies. I swear I'm big enough to sit quiet. *Pleeeeease!*" I infused my voice with as much earnest pleading as a five-year-old girl could muster and looked up at my father with Oscar-worthy puppy-dog eyes.

My dad had said he was taking Marco to the movies while Mama was at the school play rehearsal with Lessi and Maria. I was supposed to go with the girls, but that wasn't my choice. Given the opportunity, I was always at my brother's side. He was eleven, the oldest of us kids, and I idolized everything about him. If he thought it was cool to wear ankle socks, I wanted to wear ankle socks. If he went out to ride his bike, I would run along behind him as long as he would let me. As far as I was concerned, my big brother hung the moon.

"Sweet girl, we're going to see a spy movie. I'm not sure you'd like it," explained my dad, trying to let me down gently.

"Yeah!" Marco said as he entered the room. "You'd be pretty scared, Sof. This one's got guns and lots of action. It's not really a girl movie."

My face immediately pinched with annoyance. "I watch lots of movies with you, Marco. I'm not scared!"

Daddy chuckled as he patted my head. "Alright, Sof, you win. Grab your jacket, and we'll head out. We have one quick stop to make before the movie starts."

It may have only been early November, but it felt like Christmas morning to me. I bolted up to my room to grab my yellow jacket and put on my red sneakers. As I was headed out of my room, I caught sight of Maria in her room with one of Mama's candles. Stunned, I watched as she burned a small piece of paper, then lifted one of Lessi's dolls and held its beautiful golden hair to the flame.

"I'm gonna tell!" I called out from the doorway, knowing Maria would be in *big* trouble. She might be nine already, but she still wasn't allowed to play with Mama's candles, and she certainly wasn't allowed to burn Alessia's doll.

She didn't balk or chase after me. Maria just looked up and curled her finger at me. "Come here, Sofia. I want to tell you something."

Cautiously curious, I stepped inside her room. She was the oldest of us girls and claimed to be too old to play with Alessia and I. It didn't bother us too much because she could be a little mean. Maria mostly kept to herself or Marco, so she was a mystery to me. When she called me over to talk to her, I was unable to resist hearing what she had to say.

"Have you ever heard anyone say 'snitches get stitches'?" she asked coolly.

I shook my head, eyes wide as I gaped at my oldest sister.

"It means when you tell on someone, that person will hurt you for getting them in trouble. What do you think I'm going to do if you tell on me?" She lifted her brows, giving me a chance to imagine all the nasty things she was capable of. "And it's even worse when you tell on family, then you're a rat, a traitor. You see something you're not supposed to, you keep your mouth shut or bad things are gonna happen to you. Understand?" She glared at me, making tears burn at the back of my throat.

Maria could be all kinds of mean when she wanted to be. I didn't want her angry with me, so I nodded, unable to speak.

"Good, I'd hate for your paints to accidentally get thrown away or your pretty golden hair to get chopped off in the night." Her cold gray stare gave me no doubt she'd do it. I didn't know why my older sister didn't seem to like us—that was just the way she was—and I had no desire to make it worse.

I ran straight for Marco and the safety of his company, my lips sealed about what I'd seen. "I'm ready for the movies!" I said, giving him a big hug and trying to forget what Maria had said.

He chuckled, then ruffled my hair. "Alright, let's get in the car."

When Mama drove, she made Marco sit in the back seat with us girls, but Daddy let him sit up front. That meant I sat by myself in the back seat. It didn't bother me at all, as long as I got to go with them. Daddy drove us to one of his friend's houses not too far from ours. I couldn't recall ever visiting the place before, but I wasn't great at paying attention.

When we stepped out of the car, Daddy's lips pursed together just like they did when Maria got in trouble at school or when Lessi cried about something silly. I glanced around, wondering what had bothered him, but saw nothing out of the ordinary. Walking over to where I stood in the grass, he squatted down until we were eye to eye.

"I have a little business to handle, but it shouldn't take long. You run around to the backyard and play for a few minutes. I'll grab you when I'm done."

"Is Marco coming with me?" I asked with more quiver in my voice than I had wanted. I liked to be brave in front of Marco but going off by myself made me nervous.

"Marco's going to come with me, but you're not old enough. I need for you to play in the backyard for a bit while we're inside."

I could feel tears building in my eyes at the frustration of being left behind. As the youngest, it felt like I was always being left out. "I don't want to go in the backyard. I want to stay with you two."

Marco stepped forward and placed his hands on my shoulders, bending low to look me in the eye. "Hey, Sof, don't get upset," he said softly. "It's only a few minutes, and you're gonna love the yard. I've been back there, and there's tons of flowerbeds. I bet you can find a whole army of ladybugs." He gave me a warm smile, and his words were just what I needed to hear. I adored hunting for ladybugs with him. In the blink of an eye, the backyard became a grand adventure rather than a punishment for being too young.

"Okay, Marco! And maybe I can find one of the yellow ones just for you."

"Sounds good. You can tell me all about it as soon as we're done."

"And Sof," Daddy said, "make sure you stay in the backyard until we come for you, understand?"

"I will!" I tore off around the side of the house, completely absorbed in my new mission to capture as many ladybugs as possible. Daddy had been right—the yard was huge. Our house sat on the edge of the water, so we didn't have much of a backyard, but this yard was lined around the edges with trees that soared high into the sky, just like an impenetrable barrier protecting a beautiful castle. At the base of the trees were winding flower beds full of all kinds of plants and flowers. I ran directly toward the nearest bed. Ladybugs loved flowers. Dropping to my knees, I started to scour the leaves and dirt for any trace of red or yellow polka-dotted bugs.

"Whatcha lookin' for?" a voice from behind me said, startling me from my task. A boy about my age peered over my shoulder, shaggy blond hair curling into his narrowed eyes.

I'd never seen the boy before, but I was always happy to make new friends. "Ladybugs. Wanna look with me?"

"I thought girls didn't like bugs."

"They're *lady*bugs," I explained in exasperation. *Clearly, this boy didn't know anything about girls.* Of course, we liked ladybugs—it was right there in the name. I returned to my search, sensing the boy join me when he dropped to his knees beside me. "You live here?" I asked him without taking my eyes from the miniature jungle of vegetation.

"Nah, this place is way nicer than my house. My dad's

inside talking. He made me come out here." He grumbled the last part, his displeasure obvious.

"Same here. They said I wasn't old enough to come inside, but this is way better than listening to grown-ups talk."

"You're probably right," he admitted reluctantly. "How old are you?"

"Five and a half. How old are you?"

"Six, almost seven," he said proudly, flashing a toothless grin. "Hey! There's one." He reached into a large shrub and came away holding his finger out with a tiny red bug walking across his knuckle. "Wanna hold it?"

I gave him a big smile and nodded, too excited to talk.

"Okay, hold out your hand flat, and we'll let him walk from my hand to yours."

I followed his instructions, and he pressed his hand firmly against mine on the side where the ladybug was headed. My hand was frigid compared to his, but it didn't faze me. I was too excited to care about the cold or the rock that was digging into my knee. The moment the microscopic legs touch my skin, I gasped with a giggle. "It tickles."

"Have you held one before?"

"Yeah, but it still makes me laugh. I wish I got to hold them more. We don't have a big yard, so I don't see them very often. My favorite are the yellow ones, but they're super hard to find. I've only ever found one of those before. I like them because yellow is my favorite color. You have a favorite color?" I asked as I watched the bug make its way around to the underside of my hand.

"Probably green. That's the color of the New York Jets, my dad's favorite team."

"You know if you mix yellow and blue, it makes green? I

love painting, so I know how to make all the colors," I explained confidently. "Yellow and red together make orange."

The boy cocked his head to the side and looked at me curiously. "You think if the red ladybugs and yellow ladybugs have babies together, they'd have orange ladybugs?"

I burst out laughing, making the bug on my hand fly off toward more stable ground. "You're funny. What's your name?"

"I'm Nico. What's yours?"

I didn't have to answer. My dad's booming voice called my name from the side of the house. "Gotta go! I'll see ya around."

"Bye, ladybug girl." The words followed me as I ran toward my daddy, but I hardly heard them in my excitement to get back to the car.

Daddy drove us to the movie theater to see the spy movie. I sat between him and Marco so I could sit next to both of them, which meant I got to hold the popcorn. I only had to go to the potty one time during the movie and didn't get scared at all.

By the time the movie was over, it was dark outside and *way* past my bedtime. I could hardly keep my eyes open from the excitement of the day, and the car's gentle motion on the drive home quickly lulled me to sleep. I didn't wake when the doors to the car opened and closed. It was the stillness and the silence that stirred me from sleep. Blinking my groggy eyes, I quickly realized I was alone in the car. From where I sat in my booster seat, I could see Daddy and Marco outside, walking over to two men dressed in black vests. They didn't look like any men I'd seen before with their long, scraggly beards and black tattoos on their necks and faces. But my daddy wasn't scared of them, so I wasn't. My daddy had all kinds of friends.

The men shook hands under a streetlight, my brother pretending to be one of the adults. Just before my eyelids could drift shut again, the scene suddenly fell into chaos, stirring me wide-awake. Frozen in my seat, I watched my worst nightmare play out before me like a movie with no pause or rewind buttons.

One of the men in vests began to yell. I could hear his angry voice penetrate inside the car. His face contorted, and he grabbed Marco by the hair, pressing a gun to my brother's head. The man snarled at my daddy like the neighbor's dog did when we walked by the fence. My daddy stood motionless, hands raised in surrender.

Why wasn't Daddy helping Marco? Why was the man so angry?

I wasn't sure what was happening, but I could tell it was bad. My stomach clenched viciously as fear immobilized my body.

The next moment played out in slow motion, like the cartoons where the tomcat accidentally runs into a wall when he chases the little mouse. A loud bang rang out in the night, echoing off the tall buildings and making me clasp my hands over my ears. My eyes jerked shut, but only for a second. They opened in plenty of time to see Marco's head jerk to the side and a dark liquid spray out around him.

I couldn't stop what I was seeing.

As if someone was forcing my eyelids open, I watched in horrified silence as my brother's limp body collapsed to the ground, a dark puddle quickly seeping out from beneath him.

I couldn't breathe.

All the air in the car had been sucked out, making my head spin and my vision blur.

Everything stilled.

The men seemed just as shocked as me, eyes all locked on my brother.

Without warning, Daddy launched himself at the men, stealing the man's gun and hitting them both with it over and over. He attacked them like a wild animal. I could almost have convinced myself the whole thing was a scene from the movie we'd just watched. How else could my daddy be fighting like one of the spies on the big screen?

The bad men tried to hurt him, and I wanted desperately to scream for them to stop, but I couldn't make a sound. It wouldn't have mattered. Daddy was quicker than either of them, punching and kicking, pounding on the men until both were on the ground unmoving, and still he kept at them.

Eventually, he slowed, his chest heaving up and down as he glared at the men, then lowered himself to look at one of their hands. When he stood back up, he spat on each of them and turned to Marco. Daddy walked slowly to my brother's side and dropped to his knees, placing his hands gently on Marco's chest and bowing his head, but Marco never moved.

Why isn't he moving? Why isn't Daddy taking Marco to the doctor? Why is Daddy crying? Questions and panic raced through my mind, but even at five years old, I knew the answers.

I knew that my big brother was dead.

I simply couldn't face it.

My entire world had shattered, but I was in shock.

Daddy stood and pulled out his phone, making a call before returning to the car. He thought I was asleep. I wasn't supposed to have seen what happened. I knew that like I knew my own name. What I'd seen had been very, very bad. Without a second thought, I slammed my eyes closed. I didn't want him to know that I'd been awake and wanted to hide from everything that had happened. If I closed my eyes, maybe when I opened them, I would discover it had all been a mistake.

I could feel his gaze on me as I sat there motionless, head resting against the seat. I pretended to sleep, desperately hoping it was all a bad dream.

But it wasn't a dream or even a nightmare.

We sat silent in the car for a short while until another car arrived. In the heavy darkness, Daddy never saw the streaks of tears soaking my face. He rolled down the window, whispering softly to the men from the other car. Then we drove away, leaving Marco on the cold city sidewalk.

I never saw my big brother again.

CHAPTER 2

Sofia

NOW

For as long as I could remember, I'd felt like an imposter. I looked like Sofia Genovese, and everyone believed I was her, but only I knew that Sofia had died many years ago.

Perhaps that was a little dramatic.

A part of the old Sofia was still present—she showed herself in every conversation I had with my parents—but she didn't feel real. She was the mask I wore to cover up everything else I hid inside. But with each passing day, every birthday and milestone, she made fewer and fewer appearances. As I stepped out of The October Company art gallery where I would be working at my first real job, I could envision the day when I might be free to be myself around the people who were supposed to be closest to me—my family.

The thought had me smiling as I greeted the familiar face waiting for me outside.

"What are you doing here?" I asked Michael as I approached where he leaned against his parked car. "Just because you helped me get this job doesn't mean you need to follow me to work. I'm a fully capable adult," I teased wryly. Anyone else probably would have slunk away from the man, let alone teased him, but I'd known Michael for years. The menacing glare and tattoos creeping up from beneath his collar didn't scare me. Quite the opposite—the sight of his ripped jeans and scuffed boots made me feel at ease. When he was near, nothing and no one could hurt me.

He raised one of his brows, then snagged my wrist as soon as I was within reach. Wrapping his solid arm around my neck, he put me in a headlock and tousled my hair to total disarray. "Such a gracious and humble adult, aren't you?"

I wailed playfully, pinching his flat stomach through his fitted T-shirt. "Okay, you're right. I give!"

With my cry for mercy, Michael released me, and I lifted my head to find his face lit with an infectious grin. "That's better. Now, tell me how it went."

"It went really well! Miles seems like he'll be wonderful to work with, and the part-time schedule gives me plenty of time to paint." I was offered the administrative position a week before but had needed to fill out employment paperwork and discuss job duties more thoroughly. My short visit with the gallery owner had confirmed my initial impression that the locally owned operation was going to be a perfect fit.

"I've known Miles for a few years now. I knew you'd like him."

"Yeah, and working in a gallery—seeing new exhibits, meeting the artists, and planning events— doesn't even sound like work. The only thing better is painting itself!"

He gave me a smirk and a flick of his head. "Let's grab some coffee, and you can tell me all about it," he said, motioning down the sidewalk.

"Actually, I have to run over to campus to get my last couple of boxes." I smiled up at him and gave a soft punch to his shoulder. "I really do appreciate your help with the job. The gallery is amazing. I can't wait to start next week."

"You know I'm always happy to help. Speaking of, you need a hand with boxes?"

"Nah, I only have two boxes left. They didn't fit in the car on the last trip. Once I grab those, I'm all moved out of the dorm."

"Your dad and his ridiculous rules," he scoffed. "There was no reason you had to stay all four years in the damn dorm."

"I know, but that's in the past. Good things are on the horizon … I can feel it."

Michael huffed out a laugh before wrapping me in his arms. "Alright, you little ray of sunshine. Your optimism is hurting my eyes. Go get your boxes and let me know if you need help."

"Will do. Thanks again!" I waved as he slid into his black Mercedes, then pulled away from the curb.

Michael was amazing. He was the big brother I should have had—protective, indulgent, and honest to a fault. He was there for me when I needed him, and that had meant the world to me. He was also gorgeous, but our relationship had never gone down that particular path. Right at six feet tall, he was a dichotomy of striking features and an intimidating countenance, making people unsure if they should stare or look away. His disheveled hair was almost black, and his deep-set eyes were equally as dark. With full lips and hardly any facial hair, he could have been an emo model or a bad-boy musician covered in angry tattoos.

To me, he was just Michael.

He was the boy who was so fascinated with fast cars that he snuck out to watch illegal street races when we were in high school. He was the person who copied off my homework and met me at an all-night diner when I'd had a bad day and needed a plate of pancakes with hot chocolate.

Michael was my best friend, but nothing more than friendship had ever developed between us.

He never made a single move to change the status of our relationship. It was hardly an option early on. When we met, I had been devastated after a brutal breakup with a boy who had owned my heart since I was five years old. Nico had broken my heart so thoroughly that I wasn't sure it would ever work properly again. Michael helped me see that life would continue even if Nico wasn't by my side. Once I was able to see the light at the end of the tunnel, a platonic dynamic had been established between us. I cherished our friendship and had no desire to risk losing it. Michael was the one good thing that came from that time period.

If it hadn't been for Nico leaving, I probably never would have met Michael.

For the past seven years, he'd been my closest confidant and friend. He had given me so much, and now I could add my job to the list of ways he had made my life better. I glanced back at the vinyl lettering of the gallery name plastered across the window above the door. My lips pulled back involuntarily into a wide smile as warmth flooded my chest. Things were going to be different from now on. I could feel it in every cell of my body. I had seized the reins to my life and would steer myself in the direction I saw fit, rather than be subjected to the back seat and chauffeured to places I didn't want to go.

My excitement made the spring sky that much brighter and the dirty city street almost inviting. I skipped over to the Buick I had borrowed from my mom and slipped behind the wheel. My father liked for me and my sisters to use drivers in the city, but while I'd been at college, it hadn't been necessary. No doubt that was already on his to-do list, but I would deal with it later.

The traffic on my forty-five-minute drive up to the Columbia campus was far more tolerable than normal in my current mood. I found a decent parking spot and ran inside the old dorm to retrieve the first of my two remaining boxes. When I walked back to my car with the second box, a middle-aged man in aviator sunglasses and a thin leather jacket stood with his hip leaned against my car.

I'd lived in New York my entire life and was decently equipped to handle your average oddball, but my steps still faltered at the sight of him. I wasn't a fan of confrontation, and the man gave off an aggressive vibe that instantly had me on alert.

"Excuse me," I offered with a tight smile, hoping the man would step aside and allow me to get in my car without a scene.

He slowly came off the car but stayed in my path, dropping his chin in acknowledgement. "Ma'am, my name is Detective James Breechner. You mind if I ask you a couple of questions?"

I glanced around nervously, unsure what I was searching for—a parent, a witness, maybe a video camera to suggest this was a joke. Why did a cop want to question me? Had there been an issue at the dorm? I'd been so wrapped up in finals that World War III could have started, and I wouldn't have known.

Then I was slammed with the recollection of what had happened just the day before. My mom had called in the evening to tell me after the fact that my sister Alessia had been abducted. The entire incident had only lasted a matter of hours, and by the time I was informed, she had been located and safely returned home. I hadn't had a chance to visit or even talk to her yet, so the entire event felt surreal. Mom said Alessia was doing well and explained away the incident as a random kidnapping.

There wasn't an ice cube's chance in hell anything was random about the kidnapping.

I didn't know what exactly had happened; however, I couldn't help but wonder if Alessia would have been safe had my parents not kept so many secrets from us. They were trying to protect us but keeping us in the dark only made us vulnerable.

Whatever the actual cause was behind her kidnapping, I couldn't imagine my father would have informed the police, but stranger things had been known to happen. It was within a distant realm of possibilities that the cop was investigating the incident, and I definitely wanted to do what I could to help if that was the case.

"Um, sure," I offered warily, realizing I had yet to reply. I slung the box over to my hip, so it was no longer between us and waited anxiously for his first question.

"How well do you know Michael Garin?" he asked tonelessly, sending a tendril of unease ghosting down my spine. This wasn't a random questioning about a dorm incident.

The man *had* been looking for me but not because of my sister.

"Michael? Why do you want to know about Michael?" I tried to act calm, but inside, my heart was pounding a relentless rhythm against my ribs.

"Please, just answer the question."

I couldn't see his eyes through the reflective sunglasses, but the weight of his stare was unyielding, leaving no doubt that he was taking in my every movement.

"I've known him for years. We went to school together. Can you tell me what this is about?"

"I'm not at liberty to say. Can you tell me about the nature of your relationship with Mr. Garin?"

More and more alarm bells began to sound in my head. Did he have questions about Michael, or were his questions seeking information about me? How was my relationship with Michael relevant to whatever he was investigating? My parents might have tried to keep us girls blind to their mafia dealings, but they were always clear on one thing—never, ever talk to the police. Right or wrong, I was raised to believe that the cops would twist and contort anything you said and use it against you.

My jaw clamped shut at the mental reminder, and I sucked in a cleansing breath through my nose. "If you have questions for me, I think it might be best if you spoke with my lawyer. Would you like his number?"

Detective Breechner's upper lip lifted slightly in a snarl. "Is that how we're going to play this? All I'm trying to do is have a simple conversation," he said through clenched teeth.

"I'm not playing at anything. I think it's in my best interest to remain silent, and I believe that's my option. Now please, step away from my car." I was relieved to hear my voice grow fortified with each word I spoke. He had shaken me at first with his unexpected request, but I'd eventually found my backbone.

He watched me as I placed the box in the back seat. "This conversation isn't over."

"It is for now," I replied, reaching for the driver's seat door and forcing him to step back farther as I opened the door and retreated inside my car. Pressing the ignition, I thanked God I didn't have to fiddle with a key—my shaking hands could never have handled the task.

Breechner crossed his arms over his chest and glared at me as I pulled away from the curb. I didn't know what his deal was, but I certainly wasn't sticking around to find out. I drove a few miles away until I was comfortable pulling over, then dived for my phone to text Michael.

A cop just tried to question me about you. Are you in trouble?

The conversation dots immediately jumped to life. Michael was excellent about responding to my messages, unlike some guys. **No, I'm sure it was nothing. You ok?**

Yeah, just shaken. No idea what he wanted, and I didn't give him time to tell me.

I'll bet that pissed him off.

I'd be surprised if he didn't crack a tooth. The thought made me chuckle.

Serves him right for upsetting you. Try not to worry. I'm sure it's fine.

K

You get your boxes?

Yeah.

Good. Have fun back home.

Don't remind me.

His reassuring words had eased some of my tension, but I couldn't entirely shake the bad feeling that sat heavy in my gut. Then again, maybe it was just a byproduct of his reminder about my upcoming stay with my parents. Either way, my sunshiny day now felt threatened with ominous clouds on the horizon.

AFTER TEXTING MICHAEL, I made my way to my childhood home on Staten Island. The apartment I had leased in the city wouldn't be ready for three more weeks, which left me in need of a place to stay. I had money and could have rented something short-term, but my dad had insisted I come home. He wasn't the type of man you argued with. It was simply easier to stay with my parents than to fight him on it. Plus, I wouldn't have to unpack and repack in a short amount of time. They had kept my bedroom just as it was the day I left for school, which was a little odd but handy in a pinch. Assuming I could put up with my family for three weeks, it was a no-brainer.

The problem was, my family made me crazy.

I'd intentionally stayed away as much as possible over the past four years, using school as an excuse to bow out of dinners and family gatherings. It wasn't so much the people themselves that bothered me, it was the secrets. They were insidious, poisoning every aspects of our lives until even the most fundamental parts of ourselves were blurred and fuzzy, impossible to define.

Was I innately secretive? Who knew? But I'd definitely become secretive. That was the worst part of it all—I was no better than any of them. I had secrets of my own that would rock their carefully constructed world.

Hello, hypocrisy, my old friend.

I'd known my family's darkest secrets since I was a child and kept that knowledge hidden most of my life. I never gave the smallest clue that I'd known my father was a mafia boss or how I'd discovered his involvement. As far as they were concerned, I was angelic Sofia—a sweet, artistic soul who needed to be shielded and protected from life's darker side.

Every one of us wore masks in my family.

We acted a part, keeping strictly to the script and guarding our secrets ruthlessly, and it was exhausting.

I didn't see any reason, if we'd all fallen from the same rotten tree, why we couldn't be true to one another. If it had been us against the world, then at least we would have had each other. But that wasn't the case. We were outsiders even amongst ourselves, which made for an extremely lonely existence.

When I was around them, my skin itched with the need to shed itself and show them who I truly was, and my throat burned to scream, demanding we leave the secrets behind. But I kept it all bottled up, tightly sealed in a glass jar in the depths of my being. Why didn't I just let it all out? *Be the change you want to see*, and all that jazz. I'd only been five when I first started harboring secrets and hadn't known any better at the time. As I got older and recognized the plethora of the lies around me, it was too late. Telling my truths at that point was no longer a simple unburdening—there would be consequences I wasn't willing to face.

Instead of spewing my anger and frustration, I painted. It was my only outlet and had saved me on many occasions. Because of the secrets and isolation, my parents' house never really felt like home. It was a stage where we performed, not a sanctuary where we could be ourselves. Just looking at the outer façade as I pulled into the driveway had me gnawing anxiously at my fingernails.

It was three weeks. I could survive three weeks.

I unloaded the two boxes into the garage with all my other things and locked the door. My father had begrudgingly agreed to let me store my things where Mom parked her car so I didn't have to deal with the hassle of a storage unit. I knew the minute I'd locked my things away in some run-down metal building, I'd think of something I needed to retrieve. This way, I had everything nearby, and Mom's car could surely survive the elements for three weeks.

I used the key to let myself in the side door of the house closest to the detached garage. "Hey Mom, it's me," I called out, dropping my keys on the hall tree bench.

"Oh, Sofia!" Mom said as she hurried over from the other room. "I'm so glad you're home."

"Yeah, it'll be a nice little visit," I said with a forced smile. "Is Alessia still here?"

"No," she groused. "She left earlier today, even though I wasn't happy about it. She insisted on going back to her apartment. She'll be here for Sunday dinner, but I may have to drop in sooner to check on her."

"Oh! That was quick. I had hoped I'd get to see her while she was home."

"It would have been wonderful to have both of you under one roof. I think more than anything it's boy trouble that's bothering her. Maybe you could call her. It might help to talk to her sister."

"Yeah, I'll definitely give her a call in a bit."

"Good. Now, while I have you here, I was just going over this seating chart for the graduation party and want you to have a look." She took my hand and pulled me toward the kitchen.

"I can look at it, but you know I don't care where people sit." She knew very well that not only did I not care where people sat, I had no desire to have a party at all. This was her event, and I had little to do with it. However, I hadn't refused her request to throw a party, so it was my own fault that I had to deal with her incessant planning. She lived for these things, and I hated to take that from her.

My mom wasn't a bad woman; in fact, there were a lot of qualities about her that I respected. She was more apt than anyone in the family to call things as she saw them. I'd learned some colorful language from my mother over the years. One time, she cussed out a cop so thoroughly the man had blushed.

Mom was an only child in an Italian family, which is a rarity. I got the feeling she was lonely growing up, and family gatherings were her favorite social outlet. As soon as she was old enough to host, parties became her chosen pastime. She eventually spread her wings and began to use her talents for the better good by organizing charity events. It helped reduce the number of family affairs, so we were all supportive of her endeavors.

The woman came alive at the thought of hosting an event, so aside from a few grumblings under my breath, I hadn't fought her over the party. One hundred and fifty of our closest friends and family would be joining us to celebrate my graduation.

I was dreading every minute of it.

"Look here. I got Vica moved with her *guest* over to the Watters' table," she explained as she handed me a chart of tables covered with tiny scribbled names. "They own that little bar down in SoHo—the Black Horse or the Purple Pig— something like that. I hear they're swingers, so it should be fine to put Vica with them. You never know what that woman's gonna say, and I'd rather not worry about her sitting with anybody important."

I only half listened to her prattle on as my eyes flitted from one table to the next, hardly registering the names until one particular name grabbed my attention. "Ma, why is Nico's name on here?" I glared at her incredulously, but she wouldn't meet my eyes.

"Don't call me that. You know I hate it."

"*Ma*," I ground out, still waiting for an explanation.

"You were friends for a long time." She shrugged, suddenly taking the paper from my hands. "This party is for you; I wanted to have your friends there." Her tone was overly inno- cent as she tried to gift wrap what was clearly an overstep of her bounds.

"We haven't been friends for years—you *know* that." I was furious with her and barely able to contain my anger. Seeing his name had instantly conjured images of his face, contorted with disgust and contempt from the last time we spoke. I had assumed it was a phase or some kind of misunderstanding— that he would get over whatever had upset him—and things would go back to normal.

That was seven years ago.

Nothing was ever the same after that day.

Mom looked over at me with apologetic eyes. "I'm sorry, baby girl. You know I didn't mean to upset you."

I released a long, resigned sigh, my anger quickly dissipating at her remorse. "I know, Mom. I'm sure it'll be fine. He probably won't even show up." It was the truth. I hadn't run into him in seven years, so what were the chances he would actually show up to a party in my honor?

Mom gave a tight smile that looked suspiciously like guilt, but before I could question her, she changed the subject. "Let's go dress shopping, just you and me. I have time tomorrow, and we haven't done something together in so long. We can shop and have lunch. We'll find you something perfect to wear to your party!"

Oh, hell.

My mother's idea of the perfect dress was something akin to what Cinderella wore to the ball. My sense of style and hers did not mesh, but she was so excited, I couldn't find the words to refuse. "Yeah, we can do that."

"Wonderful! And I opened the sunroom and started to set up your old studio so you can paint while you're here." She paused, and her eyes took on a weary sadness. "I never thought I'd say this, but I miss having your paint all over the house."

I was her youngest—the baby of the family—and she experienced a deep sense of loss when she became an empty nester. That first year I was at Columbia, she hosted a dozen parties to keep herself busy. Since then, she had settled into the next phase of her life and was satisfied so long as we all showed up for weekly dinners.

"That's sweet, Mom. Thanks." I walked to her outstretched arms, and she wrapped me in a warm hug.

"We're glad you're home, even if it is just for a few weeks. How about you get settled in and let me know if there's anything I've forgotten, okay?"

"Yeah, sounds good." I kissed her cheek and headed for the stairs. My sisters and I had our bedrooms on the second floor along with a fourth room that had been our older brother's. That door always remained shut, which had probably made it harder to forget than if my parents had simply emptied the room and dedicated it to another purpose. Instead, it was a constant memorial to what we'd all lost.

I'd walked the path to my room a million times in my life, and it was hard not to feel like the lost little girl I'd once been as I retraced those same steps. It was precisely why I never went up there after I moved out. Even when I stopped in on Sunday for our obligatory family dinners, I stuck to the ground floor. Seeing the closed door was hard enough on my battered heart, but the reminder of Nico was more than it could take. Rather than unpack, I curled beneath the covers of my double bed and allowed the strong hands of grief to drag me down beneath the surface of its icy waters.

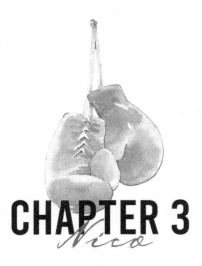

CHAPTER 3
Nico

NOW

E veryone in the outfit had been on edge for the past twenty-four hours after Alessia Genovese was kidnapped. Word got around when she'd been located, but tensions were still elevated to a stifling degree. Shit behind the scenes must have been bad because Alessia's father, Enzo Genovese, stepped out of the shadows for the first time and took ownership of his role as boss of the Lucciano family.

My boss.

I was sworn member of his outfit—whether I had wanted to be or not.

Now, it was an accepted part of my life, but that hadn't always been the case. Once I was initiated, I had no choice but to accept my fate and settle into my role as a soldier in the organization. I was a grunt and well aware of it, which was why it surprised me to receive a summons to attend a meet.

Soldiers were pawns. Our capos gave us our marching orders, and that was generally as far up the chain as we had contact. When I stepped into the Manhattan conference room at a building I'd never been to before, I was stunned to find myself in a room full of capos along with Enzo Genovese himself. I only knew two men in the room by sight—my capo, Gabe, and a longtime friend, Tony Pellegrini, who was already seated on the opposite side of the room. He gave me a lopsided smile and a chin lift but stayed seated. I didn't know any of the other men, but judging by their age and expensive clothes, I was likely the only soldier in the room.

I tried to keep the tension from coiling in my shoulders— guys like these could smell unease—but it was hard when I had no fucking clue what I was doing there. Gabe had greeted me when I entered the room, but I hadn't been given any other information or instruction. Resorting to my normal MO, I took a seat in one of the chairs along the wall of the room and sat back to observe.

My dad was a degenerate gambler, and his worthlessness had colored my perceptions of the outfit when I discovered he was a member. It didn't take me long once I'd been taken into the fold to realize there was a lot more to the life than my father. Every corner of the Earth had its share of addicts and miscreants. But in the family, those guys never made it past the bottom rung—soldiers, if they were lucky, but many were only ever associates. The room was full of successful businessmen, powerful and well-established in the organization, and I had no idea what the fuck I was doing there.

"Alright fellas, let's get started." Enzo didn't have to holler over the murmur of voices to seize the attention of everyone in the room. At his simple command, the room went silent as a mortuary, and all eyes turned to where Enzo stood at the head of the table. "As everyone here has heard, we recently suffered an unforgiveable betrayal. My trusted underboss, Sal Amato, set my daughter and me up to be killed and has been sullying the family name, angling for a war. He attempted to use my anonymity to usurp my role as boss. Everyone here knows that we prize secrecy above all else to protect ourselves and our families, but my removed presence left us vulnerable from within. I say 'us' because this wasn't just an attack on me. Sal's actions have affected us all." His searing gaze swept the room as he addressed the group, his voice resounding with certainty. "We don't call meetings like this anymore because it's not safe to have us all in one place, but this needed to happen, if only for a few minutes. Things are going to change. I want every one of you to hear it straight from my mouth. I'm taking this outfit back."

He didn't get another word out before the room erupted in cheers. I joined the group in clapping for the return of strong leadership in our organization. Although the same man was still in charge, it made an enormous difference with how we were perceived when our leader stood proudly front and center. I might not have been the typical goodfella, but I was a part of the outfit for life, and I had no desire to see it run by a man hiding in the shadows.

"As the first matter of business moving forward," Enzo continued, quieting the crowd. "I'm pleased to name Gabe Fiore as my new underboss." He gestured to Gabe who stood from his place at the table to clasp Enzo's hand. It was clear this wasn't news to Gabe, and I silently cursed the man for not giving me a heads-up.

While the room clapped in congratulations, my hands

involuntarily followed suit, but my mind raced to grasp the implications. Before I could get far, I was drawn from my thoughts at the sound of my name.

"Antonico Conti," Enzo announced, all eyes landing on me. "Normally, these matters are handled on a smaller stage, but I wanted all my capos present today. Going forward, you will take on Gabe's previous role in the outfit as capo."

I hadn't been caught off guard in years, but his words had my heart stuttering in my chest. Hands patted my back warmly in congratulations, and I dropped my chin toward Enzo in acknowledgement of the honor he was bestowing upon me. The day had started out like any other, but I could hardly believe how vastly my life had just changed with the utterance of a few words.

Capo.

I'd been named a capo in the Lucciano family.

Considering the bumbling legacy my father had established for me, I wasn't sure I'd ever be considered for such a promotion. I would now outrank my father. Pride expanded in my chest and bubbled up until I couldn't force down the smile that spread across my face. Not many men were selected at such a young age for advancement. Being named a capo was a remarkable honor, and I had every intention of proving myself worthy of the position.

I had to force myself to set aside my racing thoughts and listen to Enzo as he continued.

"We haven't been able to corner Sal, but we will. I promise you," he said with steely conviction. "In the meantime, I'll be working hard to improve our relationship with the Gallos and the other families, along with other organizations."

The Lucciano and Gallo families had a long history of bad

blood between them. Recently, Sal had stoked those fires further by having the Gallo Consigliere's son killed and framing Enzo. While Sal's treachery had been explained to the Gallos, it hadn't fully eased the tension. The two families carried enough baggage through the years that even a small slight would be taken as a major offense, let alone the death of an important family member. We were lucky war hadn't broken out.

"In particular, we're facing a major problem with the Russians. Yesterday, two of our soldiers were sent back to us with a message about a deal we have allegedly backed out of, so we'll have to figure out what Sal's done and find a way to smooth things over." A message was a polite way of saying they'd been beaten half to death. The Russians were fucking ruthless and only slightly less crazy than the Irish. It was never a good idea to cross either of them.

Not wanting to push our luck by keeping everyone in one room for too long, Enzo finished his speech and closed out the meeting in a matter of minutes. I received several more congratulations on my way out and was introduced to some of the men I'd never met. The older men easily accepted me into the fold, and I was relieved to be so well received.

So why in the hell did the meeting leave me wanting to put my fist through somebody's face?

The entire time I sat there, agitation bubbled up inside me like water in a boiling pot. It wasn't until an hour later when I was taking out that unprovoked emotion on my sparring partner, Leo, when I finally caved and accepted the reason behind my anger. Seeing Enzo had taken me back to the lowest point in my life. He was a stark reminder of everything

I'd lost. Not just the life I'd lost, but *her*—Enzo's daughter, Sofia.

Seeing him reminded me of her.

Thoughts of her weren't necessarily uncommon, but I no longer suffered the crushing anger and regret that came along with them. At least, not until I looked at Enzo and recognized her same hazel eyes in his. I had thought the emotions brought on from our separation had finally dissipated.

Clearly, I'd been mistaken.

It appeared all I'd done was bury the anguish deep inside me. One look at him, and it all came rushing back to the surface like water bursting through a dam.

I shot my fist out in a wicked left cross that caught Leo on the chin.

His head flew to the side, and he took a steadying step back. "Jesus, man! You tryin' to break my jaw? I thought we were sparring here." He took off his glove and massaged his face, the swelling already setting in.

I let out a long sigh, my eyes drifting up to wander along the dusty rafters. "Shit, I'm sorry. I have a lot on my mind and got carried away."

"I think you need to get back in the ring. When's the last time you fought?" Leo leaned himself against the ropes, sweat dripping from his short blond hair down into his eyes.

"It's been a while. Guess I may not be doing that anymore … not sure. They made me capo today." I removed my gloves and began to unwind the wraps from my hands without looking up at my longtime friend.

"The *fuck*? And you're just telling me *now*?" He was giving me a hard time, but I could hear the excitement in his voice.

I raised my eyes to peer at him, the corner of my lip lifting in a smirk.

Leo charged at me, wrapping his arms around my middle and hoisting me in the air with a whoop. "I knew my boy was gonna make it. You're in the bigtime now!"

"Put me down, dickhead," I barked on a laugh.

Leo dropped me before nailing me in the shoulder. "That's great news, so what's with all the attitude? How come you were pissed enough you almost took my head off?"

I bent between the ropes and dropped down to the ground outside the ring. "Seeing Enzo just brought back a lot of shit I didn't want to think about."

"Ah, Sofia," he mused knowingly.

"They fucked with my entire life. It's not just her." I wasn't sure which one of us I was trying to convince.

Judging by his smirk, Leo wasn't buying it any more than I was. "Whatever you say, boss."

"Don't you start calling me that."

"Call you what?" asked Kayla Barone, one of the resident gym bunnies as well as one of my go-to stress relievers. Her toned body could have graced the cover of *Women's Fitness*, and she wasn't shy about showing it off. Not only was she highly sexual, but she craved the attention.

I met Kayla before I started training at Joe's Gym. It was a couple of years after I'd been made, and her father had introduced us at a party. We were celebrating some birthday or holiday—I couldn't even remember what the bullshit excuse was—but a number of us had gathered to sip on gold-label drinks in fancy clothes. I hated going to those things, but it was a part of the business. Kayla was wearing a silver tube-sock of a dress that barely covered the bottom of her ass cheeks. She had batted her eyes and giggled at me enough times to convey she was fair game, but her father was a capo, and there was no way I was going to sign my own death certificate. When I wouldn't take the bait, she went so far as to lean over a chair and expose her bare pussy to me. I left the party as quickly as I could before I did something stupid. It wasn't until I started going to Joe's and heard about Kayla playing hokey pokey with half the guys there that I gave in. She'd proven good for a quickie in the locker room or acting as a plus-one should I need a no-strings date. Kayla definitely had her uses, but nothing about her appealed to me on a deeper level.

No woman had since Sofia.

"I called him boss. This guy was just named capo," offered Leo with a pat on my shoulder as he made his way to the locker room. Ordinarily, we didn't discuss that shit in public, but our gym was family owned. Everyone there was connected in one way or another, even Kayla.

Her face lit with a wide, ultra-white grin, and she pressed her body up against mine, her hands resting on my chest. "That's amazing news," she offered in a husky purr. "I'd love to celebrate with you if you're ... *up* for it." She peered up at me from beneath her fake lashes and pressed her rounded silicon breasts against me. Her enhancements weren't my ideal, but they didn't keep me from getting a stiffy in the middle of the gym.

"Didn't you start seeing Caleb a while back?" I wasn't particularly close with him, but he was a decent guy.

She gave a small shrug. "It's not like we're married. What he doesn't know isn't gonna hurt him. This is a celebration after all."

"I'll pass." I stepped back, grabbing a towel off a nearby bench, and started toward the locker rooms.

"That's where you're gonna draw the line? You suddenly a Goody Two-shoes?" she shot back, incensed at being rebuffed.

"Everyone has lines. Mine may be fucked up, but they're there," I called back over my shoulder.

"You don't have lines. I know you, Nico Conti. You're not fooling anyone."

I didn't look back because I had no response. I wasn't about to argue over my rightful place on the spectrum of good and evil. She might have thought she knew me, but she didn't know the half of it. There was no question in my mind I'd be situated firmly between rotten and unforgivable.

What did it say about me that I wouldn't fuck around behind a friend's back? Nothing. I was still a criminal. I'd done horrible things in my short life; some that made me feel like the most depraved sort of monster. The images of the things I'd done refused to be forgotten. They regularly haunted my dreams in graphic detail, reminding me that I had solidified my seat in hell.

Some might argue I was redeemable because I could determine the difference between right and wrong. I disagreed. I firmly believed it was that very knowledge that was my damnation. A psychopath is sick. They see no black and white, right or wrong. They don't know any better. But a man like me, I know the difference, and I hurt people anyway.

That was the definition of evil.

IF SEEING Enzo was an unwelcome trip down memory lane, getting a summons later that day to meet with him at his home was a fucking nightmare. I had no idea what he wanted to speak with me about, but when the boss calls, you go, no matter how much you dread it.

Seeing that house again was a serious punch to the nuts—it literally winded me as I walked to the front sidewalk. I hated the emotions that stirred inside me at just seeing the place. It had been years since I'd walked up the steep steps to the front door.

I had truly believed I'd never go there again.

Up until this week, Enzo had kept his identity secret. Even though he was my boss in the outfit, I'd had no reason to see his face or speak his name. My discovery of his role had been an accident on the night of my initiation—my sixteenth birthday. I'd caught sight of him outside a window and known he was involved.

For most kids, their sixteenth birthday is one of the best days of their lives. For me, it was the day my life ended. Not only did I lose my innocence but I'd also lost everything good in my life on that one night. But that was a long time ago. I'd made peace with how my life had unfolded, and I was a different person now. I'd made a name for myself and moved on. I'd survived just fine without *her*, despite the raging emotions I'd felt at the time. I was a teenager in mourning, certain the world had come to an end. Now that I was on the other side, I had no intention of burying myself in that same emotional sandpit.

As I rang the doorbell, I sucked in a lungful of crisp evening air and admonished myself to remember that I was no longer that pubescent teen.

"Nico, it's good to see you. Come in." Enzo opened the door, extending his hand in greeting.

"It's good to see you too, Mr. Genovese."

"Let's go back to my office and talk."

I follow him to a large formal office not far off the entry. He closed the door behind us, and I breathed a small sigh of relief at making it inside without any drama. The room was filled with a lifetime of books and memorabilia tastefully displayed on shelves and in glass curios. He bypassed the plaid wingback chairs in a small seating area and instead took his place behind an impressive mahogany desk. I sat opposite him in one of the leather desk chairs and tried not to show my unease.

"I hope this wasn't an inconvenience. I know it was short notice," he offered respectfully. That was why Enzo had risen as far as he had. He didn't leash his men with fear or abuse them like an asshole. The Lucciano boss was exceedingly savvy. He understood the importance of respect and honor while exercising his power over those who followed him. Despite his anonymity, his leadership style was felt down the ranks. His increased presence would only add to the dignity of our outfit.

"Not at all. I'm honored to be here," I responded easily.

"Good, good. I have an important matter I want to discuss with you. But first, I want to congratulate you on being named capo."

"Thank you, sir. It was an unexpected honor."

"When I spoke with Gabe about becoming my underboss, he was quick to recommend you for his replacement. You've shown remarkable dedication, drive, and intelligence. With so much of our business concentrated in online pursuits, I think it's important for us to have plenty of young blood in our ranks. Us old-timers aren't as savvy on the newest technology. Guys like you and Tony can bring your ideas to the table and be a great asset to our organization."

"This outfit is my life. I'll do whatever I can to serve the family."

"That's good to hear because I have a sensitive matter for you. As you heard earlier today, we have a number of difficult issues we are dealing with at the moment, making our lives significantly more dangerous than they've been in recent years. Now that I've come back into the limelight, my family will make for easy targets. Alessia, Maria, and my wife all have protection, but Sofia is a different matter. I know you two went your separate ways, but it's been years now, and I'm hoping you can mend that broken fence.

"She has no knowledge of our family activities, and I see no reason that needs to change, which makes security for her a bit of an issue. She won't understand why she needs to be protected and would likely resist the intrusion. I'm hoping, perhaps, if her bodyguard was a childhood friend, we could play off your role as merely a reunion of sorts—an old friend come back into her life."

The longer he spoke, the louder the ringing sounded in my ears. Surely, it had interfered with my hearing, and I had misunderstood him. He had to have known I'd broken his daughter's heart, and there was no way she would welcome me back in her life.

This can't be happening.

The words repeated over and over in my head, but it didn't matter how many times I heard them, Enzo's intentions were clear. He wanted me to guard Sofia. I wasn't sure if the concept made me more terrified or pissed. Walking away from her had been one of the hardest things I'd ever had to do, and now, I was expected to open that wound and possibly go through the whole process again.

What shit had I done in my past lives to deserve this?

It must have been supremely fucked up because this had to be a punishment.

I tried to remind myself that I was being presumptive. The assignment wouldn't be all that difficult if Sofia and I could be casual friends. We had both grown up since I walked away, and time would have lessened the hurt.

I was so full of shit.

What I'd done to her was unforgivable.

The only explanation for Enzo entertaining this scenario was if he didn't know. There was no way if she'd told him what I'd done that he'd still want me near his youngest daughter.

Fuck.

My mind raced with panicked thoughts as Enzo continued. "She's living with us for the next couple of weeks and will be protected under my roof. I want you to use that time to get reacquainted so that when she moves to her new apartment, you have a reason to stay near her. Usually this type of job would be delegated to a soldier, but considering all the circumstances, I think you're the best fit for the job. It won't be permanent, just while we get our shit straightened out with the other families and the damn Russians. Once things settle, I'll assign her a driver who can act as her security. This may not be the normal task of a capo, but it's more important to me than any other. My family is at risk, and until things settle down, their protection is paramount. I think you, more than any other man, would protect her with your life." He smiled at me, believing he had given me a great honor, which he had. But he had no idea just how impossible the task was.

Double fuck.

How could I possibly argue my way out of my first assignment as capo? I couldn't. It was my responsibility to do my job, no matter how unrealistic it might seem. I would have to do my best to protect her from a distance because the chances were slim to none that she was going to welcome me back into her life.

"Carlotta and I will do our part to help bring you back into the picture, and we'll leave the rest up to you. When you're not actively working on this assignment in the coming weeks, Gabe will help get you up to speed on handling the books in his territory. Hopefully, with your background at the fights, you'll have a good understanding already."

"Absolutely," I assured him. At least the books were one thing I was confident I could handle. "I've worked with Gabe on his records a number of times, so it shouldn't be a problem."

"Excellent. I'm proud of you, son. I know this may all seem like a lot to take in at once, but I wouldn't have asked if I didn't think you could do it. You've impressed everyone in the organization over the past years with your dedication and loyalty. Keep it up, and I see great things in your future." He smiled at me warmly, and I forced a grin in response.

"Thank you, Mr. Genovese. I promise, I won't let you down." I stood and reached for his hand, giving it a firm shake.

"I have a few things to take care of. Are you good to let

yourself out?" If I didn't know better, I'd have said he had a mischievous gleam in his eye.

"Of course. You have a good evening." I tipped my head and made for the hallway, glancing left with the intention of turning right toward the front door. But at the sight of light coming from the end of the hall, my feet betrayed me. Rerouting my intended destination, I stepped farther down the hall toward the soft glow. I had no idea what the hell I was doing. It was like my brain had shut down and instinct had taken over. Inside the home where she grew up, I could feel Sofia's presence everywhere.

I wasn't ready to leave.

The happiest moments of my life had been spent with her, and a part of me yearned to relive them. To have that piece of my life back.

She had just graduated, and I'd been stunned when I received an invitation to her party. Now that I'd been given my assignment, it made a hell of a lot more sense. Enzo said she would be staying with them. Had she already moved back home? The light shined from the doorway of her old studio. I couldn't resist the temptation to close the short distance and peek inside the room.

What they say is true—curiosity killed the cat.

Taking those last steps was a monumental mistake, and I knew it the moment I laid eyes on her golden hair piled on her head in a messy bun. I could remember the silky texture of her hair as my fingers threaded through her long waves. I knew the soft warmth of her skin against my lips as if it had only been hours since our last kiss. I could even recall the strange tightness that spread through my chest every time she gazed up at me with an adoring smile on her face.

It wasn't just a flood of memories. I was suddenly drowning in a deluge of remembered sensations—her floral scent that clung to her hair and clothes, the sound of her squeal when I tickled her, and the way I looked forward to seeing her every day at school. The memories seized my lungs, making my chest burn in protest.

It was a good thing she stood with her back to me, lost in her painting, because I couldn't look away.

I was still totally and utterly lost for her, and it pissed me the fuck off.

I should have known my feelings would remain just as strong now as they had been back then. Sofia wasn't the type of girl you forgot. She wasn't like any other girl, period. It was easy to see in her artwork, if nowhere else. Even as a little girl, Sofia didn't paint rainbows and flowers. Her canvases portrayed flocks of screeching blackbirds or a small ship doomed in the open waters of a raging sea. In her makeshift studio, dressed in tiny shorts and a top that was falling off one shoulder, Sofia painted on a canvas depicting a pile of three skulls.

It was dark, and morbid, and breathtaking.

A part of me wondered what she would do if I were to make myself known. Would her face contort in anger as she relived the awful things I'd said and done? Would she throw her brushes at me and scream for me to leave? Or would it be even worse? Would she look at me with total indifference? The thought lodged in my throat as I stepped back from the doorway.

Regardless of what her reaction would be, I would find out soon enough.

I wasn't in a rush for judgment day.

I silently made my retreat to the front door and let myself out. After the day I'd had, I was ready to lose myself in a bottle of scotch until the memories were a blurry haze.

THE SADDLE BAR was a local joint hidden in a basement with hardly a sign to direct new traffic toward its dilapidated entry. The patrons inside were either regulars or folks who had been brought in by a regular. It was where most of the guys I knew hung out, and where I planned to spend the rest of my delightful evening drinking myself stupid.

"Well, look who's here. Haven't seen you around in a while. Started to think you found another place to drown your troubles," called the bartender as soon as I walked in.

"Petey, you know you couldn't get rid of me that easily," I shot back as I sat on a stool at the far end of the bar. Pete owned and operated the Saddle Bar and knew just about every man and woman who entered his doors. He helped them get home if needed and conveniently forgot who had been in when questioned by the authorities or angry wives. He had to be pushing seventy, but he was a stand-up guy. He made the place feel like home.

I hadn't even had a chance to take a sip of my drink when a hand clasped over my shoulder.

"Who do we have here? I'd say it's someone who just got a promotion. Congratulations, man!" Tony Pellegrini and I had been friends in grade school and were initiated around the same time. His father had been a well-respected capo, and when the man passed away, Tony took his place even though he'd been young for the position. "I figured you might be out celebrating tonight, although your little party of one here isn't exactly what I envisioned." He took a seat next to me after giving me a hug and a loud pat on the back.

"Thanks, Tone."

"Your excitement is overwhelming. Try to calm down."

"It's not that." I glanced around for eavesdroppers. "I got my first assignment tonight, and I have no idea how the fuck I'm supposed to do it," I explained, speaking softly so that we weren't overheard.

"Oh, yeah? Is it something you can talk about?"

"I wasn't told not to. Just found out tonight the boss wants me to guard Sofia. I'm supposed to swoop back into her life, make friends, and protect her without her knowing."

Tony and Leo were the only two people who had known about the Genovese girls and my past with Sofia. Leo was Alessia's bodyguard, and Tony had been a capo long enough to know the boss and his family. The two of them were the only people who would understand what a clusterfuck I'd found myself in.

Tony let out a low whistle. "Jesus, you're up shit creek." His eyebrows lifted nearly to his hairline. "Better down that drink. You're gonna need it."

We clinked our glasses and shot the amber liquid, making my chest burn in just the right way.

Tony motioned to Pete for the next round. "You seen her yet?" he asked, eyeing me warily.

"No." Sofia and I hadn't talked, so it wasn't really a lie. I didn't think Tony was asking whether I had perved on her from a distance.

"How you gonna get her to let you near her?"

"No idea," I grumbled, taking a sip of my replenished drink.

"You know, all it would probably take is an apology. Girls love that shit."

"Don't think that'll work with Sofia. She's more complex than most girls." I picked up one of the bar coasters and ran my fingers around the curved edges.

"You guys were inseparable all through school. I was there, remember? She's got to miss you just as much as you miss her."

My eyes jumped up to his. "What makes you think I miss her?"

"Because I'm not blind. It's written all over your pathetic face. Don't think I've seen you look so torn up since you broke it off with her. You loved her then, and you love her now. You don't just forget a love like that."

"Thanks for the pep talk, dickhead. It's not that simple."

"It's as simple as you want it to be."

My temples began to pulse as my frustration grew. Tony was a good friend, but right now, I wanted to put my fist through his face.

"Have you considered what would have happened if you'd just told her?" Sensing my agitation, he softened his tone, not wanting to work me up any further.

I let out a long breath of air, like steam from a tension release valve. "Of course, I did. I thought it through back then and have rehashed it countless times through the years." I couldn't tell her what I'd done because she never would have looked at me the same. Plus, it would have unveiled her father's secrets, and that could have gotten me killed. I had to leave her and make certain she didn't fight to have me back because I wasn't strong enough to resist.

If she'd pushed for long, I would have laid all my secrets at her feet.

She didn't deserve the life I led, and I didn't want to be the man who dragged her down to my level. "It wouldn't have been a fairy-tale ending, that's for sure. It went down exactly as it should have, and I'll do my job, just like I'm supposed to. Our past changes nothing."

"Well, I know it don't help, but I think it's ridiculous they didn't tell those girls."

"No, it's better this way. She can have a life outside the outfit, and there's no chance the law could ever touch her. I'd rather she was safe than mine." I downed the rest of my glass, starting to feel the telltale dulling of my senses as the alcohol began to kick in.

Behind us, the room erupted in groans and boos. The televisions in the bar were all set to a football game—the New York Jets were playing, and the quarterback had been intercepted.

"Good, I hate that fucking team," I muttered under my breath so I didn't get the shit kicked out of me.

"Hate the man, not the team," shot back Tony, aware of my dislike of anything associated with my father.

"I can't. The two feel inseparable."

"Yeah, some things are like that, I guess." He gave me a loaded look that I promptly removed from his face with my fist. My response was uncalled for, but damn did it feel good.

CHAPTER 4
Sofia

NOW

For three solid hours, my mother and I shopped for a dress. I'd just about written off our little outing as a total failure when I spotted a long black gown with a gorgeous plunging back. The dress had been accented by a chunky jeweled necklace hanging low on the back, giving the sexy look just the right amount of sophistication. My breath caught as I took in the display, eyes traveling from the thin spaghetti straps down the fitted gown to the slight flare at the hem. I wasn't sure I'd ever fallen in love with a dress like I did at that moment.

"Oh honey, it's perfect." My mother's reverent words startled me from my trance.

To humor her, I'd tried on pink tulle, head-to-toe gold sequins, and one dress covered in a beaded peacock feather mosaic. This dress was entirely opposite of everything she'd selected. I was stunned when she didn't dismiss it with hardly a look.

"I figured you'd think it was too plain," I stuttered.

"It's not plain. Its beauty is in its simplicity, and sometimes that makes the greatest statement." She gazed at me warmly as my brows creased in dismay.

Who is this woman and what did she do with my mother? Did I step into some alternate dimension?

"Alright, you can stop looking at me like I sprouted a second head. I know I had you trying on things you'd never pick, and maybe that was me being a little selfish. All my baby girls are grown up, and I couldn't help myself. But this one screams your name, so before I get teary, get in there and try it on."

I fell into my mom's arms, hugging her in a way I hadn't done in a long time. All I'd ever wanted for my family was a closeness that was always just out of reach. In these rare moments when I connected with one of them, it filled my heart with joy. If only our exchange had been the standard rather than the exception.

The dress fit beautifully, so we finished the purchase and made our way to lunch. Mom had her heart set on a French restaurant not far from where we'd been shopping at Saks on Fifth Avenue. We called her driver to pick us up and took the short trip to the restaurant, leaving the dress in the car for safekeeping.

La Grenouille was a beautiful upscale bistro bursting with fresh floral arrangements and authentic retro-French décor that made you feel as if you had flown straight to Paris. It was a bit over the top for my taste, but my mother loved the place.

We were quickly shown to our seats, and I had no more than picked up the menu when my mother greeted someone just behind me.

"Oh! What a pleasant surprise! Sofia, look who's here." Her voice sounded thin and a touch higher than normal.

I narrowed my eyes at her before turning around to greet the newcomer. I couldn't have been more stunned if I had turned to see Santa Claus himself followed by his merry elves. Nico Conti stood towering over me, arms clasped behind his back, lips curved in an easy smile.

He was the last person I would have expected to find at La Grenouille.

My mouth dropped open, but nothing came out—no words, no air—my lips simply parted like a fish stranded ashore. Not just at the shock of seeing him, but also at how much he'd changed. Nico wasn't the sixteen-year-old boy I'd last seen. At well over six feet and solid muscle, he was a fully developed man. He wore a white button-down shirt that stretched tight over his shoulders and biceps, testing the strength of the fabric. His hair was trimmed close on the sides, and his long waves on top were styled back, tamed with product to stay in place. My eyes slowly traced over each of his features, taking him in as if I was trying to memorize every square inch of him. When my gaze landed on his, I realized that his body might have changed, but his eyes were still that same deep blue I lost myself in so many years ago. I was no longer a fish gasping for air. Now, I was drowning in the raging waters of his oceanic gaze—fathomless, turbulent, and totally consuming.

"Nico," Mom went on when I failed to say a word. "We were just talking about you yesterday. How are you?"

"Is that right?" he asked smoothly, never taking his eyes from mine. "I'm doing well, thank you."

"You know what?" she said as she jumped from her chair. "I have to run to the little girl's room. Nico, have a seat so you two can catch up." She motioned him to sit before disappearing around the corner, all before I could make a single protest.

My eyes bounced back and forth between Nico and my mother's treacherous departure.

She wouldn't have—couldn't have. Could she?

It was all too convenient, and as much as I didn't want to believe it, it was rather obvious.

I'd been set up.

You have to be fucking kidding me.

Here I was, thinking of having a rare bonding moment with my mother, and she was busy stabbing me in the back. I knew she'd invited him to the party, but I never dreamed she would throw me to the wolves so entirely.

I wasn't ready. I had known it was a possibility I'd see him at the party, but I thought I was going to have time to prepare for that—plan what I'd say and practice keeping my composure. Instead, my mother had taken the rug right out from under me, sending me flailing to my ass like an idiot.

Aside from shock, I couldn't even pinpoint how I felt about seeing him. All my emotions collided and canceled each other out until nothing but shock and numbness remained, which was one small grace. It helped me pull myself together and pretend I wasn't falling apart inside.

"You'll have to excuse my rudeness. I wasn't expecting to see you here." I clasped my hands tightly in my lap, attempting not to fidget, my eyes cast anywhere but at him.

"It's good to see you, Ladybug," he offered casually as if it had been days and not years since we'd seen one another.

His voice had matured and was now a gravelly rumble that filled my stomach with a swarm of butterflies taking flight, but I hardly noticed. I was too focused on the fiery rage that heated me from the inside out. He had no right to use that name after everything he'd done. After all those years. Hot, angry tears burned at the back of my throat.

"Don't you *dare* call me that," I hissed. "I don't know what's going on here, but I don't want any part of it." I threw my napkin onto the table, but before I could stand, his hand came down on mine.

"Easy, Sofia," he soothed in a calm tone. "I'm not here to upset you."

"What other reason could you possibly have?" I scoured his features over the flickering votive candle, trying to decipher what was going on, but came up empty.

"Maybe I missed you." His words were sweet and almost sounded earnest, which was why they made me laugh.

I leaned back in my chair, yanking my hand away from his and feeling my shattered armor repairing itself in record time. "Yeah, right. After seven years, you expect me to believe you woke up this morning and decided to see what I was up to?"

"Not at all. I expect you to believe that I wake up every morning thinking about you. You don't just cross my mind; you live in it." He held my eyes with such burning intensity that my gaze fused to his.

What was he implying? How could he say such a thing after he'd cast me away like yesterday's garbage? I took in a shaky breath when my lungs screamed for air, then found the strength to drop my gaze. Every hour and every day of the interminable pain I suffered after he left crashed over me, washing away the numbness. There was no question how seeing him made me feel—it was the excruciating refracturing of a wound I'd thought long healed.

"Please, leave." It was only a whisper, and all I could muster past the aching lump in my throat. I couldn't even lift my gaze as he stood.

Nico bent to place an unexpectedly soft kiss on my forehead, his rough fingertips cupping my cheek. "I'm sorry, Sof." His rumbled words constricted themselves around my heart, making it hard to breathe as he pulled away from me.

"Nico? Are you leaving so soon?" my mother asked from nearby in a boisterous voice. "You're welcome to join us, you know."

"I appreciate the offer, Mrs. Genovese, but I have somewhere to be. Take my card. It's got my number on it. Maybe we can all get together sometime. It was lovely running into you both."

"Oh … yes, of course. Please, keep in touch." My mother reclaimed her seat and attempted to continue our luncheon as if nothing had happened, but it might as well have been a lunch for one. I couldn't force down a single bite, nor could I stand to look at her. Instead, I sipped my water and counted the delicate petals on each fragrant rose in the bouquet beside our table. I made it to seven hundred and twenty before the nightmare was over and we left for home.

One would think I would have overcome the feeling of being utterly alone. It was not the first time I'd experienced it, or even the second, and it surely would not be the last. But each time, it hurt just as profoundly as the time before. Seeing him brought back the stabbing pain of loneliness. It was ironic because when we'd first become friends, Nico was my only refuge from that very same pain.

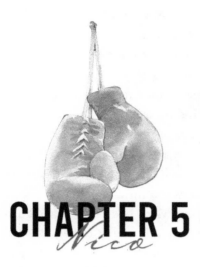

CHAPTER 5
Nico

THEN

I wasn't the same as the other kids at Xavier Catholic School. When they talked about their gaming systems and extravagant family vacations, it was easy to tell their families were different from mine. Their moms didn't work and were able to come to school for class parties. They had bouncy castles and magicians at their birthday parties. We lived in a tiny two-bedroom house and had never been on a single family vacation.

One time when my parents were fighting, I heard my dad call my school a waste of goddamn money. My mom yelled back that she didn't ask for much, and Xavier was where she drew the line. I guess Ma won the fight because they never moved me to public school.

I didn't mind Xavier. The teachers were nice, and there was a huge playground with monkey bars. I was bigger and stronger than the other boys in first grade, so I always won when we raced, especially on the monkey bars. I might not have been the same as the other kids, but being strong and fast helped me make friends.

About a week after I met the ladybug girl, I was surprised to see her sitting on a swing at my school during recess. I'd never noticed her at my school before, but there were lots of kids, and kindergarten through third grade all had recess together after lunch. She wasn't swinging; she just sat on the swing staring down at the dirt below.

"Hey, Ladybug Girl. Did you always go to my school?" I asked, coming to stand in front of her.

When she lifted her eyes to look at me, she didn't look like the same person. For a second, I wondered if I had been mistaken, but the red sneakers and yellow jacket were the same, and I was reassured that it was her.

She didn't say a word, just nodded.

"What grade are you in?" I asked out of curiosity, wondering how I'd never noticed her before.

"Kindergarten," she said in a small voice.

I wasn't sure what was wrong, but I could tell she was upset. "Are you okay?"

She thought for a minute before shaking her head.

The swing next to her was empty, so I sat down. "You want me to get a teacher?"

Again, she shook her head.

"Is there anything I can do?"

This time, when she looked at me to answer, a tear slipped down her cheek. I remembered her excitement at hunting for ladybugs and the way her smile had made me smile in return.

I wanted more than anything to bring that happiness back to her face.

"Hey, Nico! Come race me! I've been practicing and know I can beat you this time," one of the boys called out as he came to stand by the swings. Several more kids joined him, waiting for my answer.

"Nah, not right now. You guys race without me."

"Come on, Nico," pushed one of the other boys. "Don't waste your time with her. Sofia's being weird and won't talk anymore. Come play with us on the monkey bars."

I wasn't sure why his words upset me, but they made me want to shove him to the ground. "Shut up, John. I don't want to race with you guys anyway," I barked back at him with a glare.

The kids walked away mumbling "fine" and "whatever" until it was just me and the girl again. We sat quietly for a minute, just watching the other kids playing as we kicked at the loose dirt below us.

"You like to swing?" I finally asked her, not sure if she'd answer.

She looked over at me, and there was a tiny hint of light in her eyes that hadn't been there moments before as she gave me a nod. I pushed myself back and start swinging, and she did the same. We spent the rest of recess on the swings together, not saying a word.

Each day that week played out the same. When I came out to recess, she'd already be on the swings just sitting there. Once I'd join her, we'd begin to swing.

On Friday, when recess ended and we had to go back to our classes, I stopped her and gave her a small smile. "Bye, Ladybug Girl. I'll see you next week."

For the first time all week, she smiled, and my chest filled with warmth and an intense happiness I'd never known existed.

From that moment on, I was hers.

CHAPTER 6
Sofia

NOW

A fter Marco's death, I kept my mouth shut about what I'd seen. For a while, I didn't say anything at all. Not a word. They attributed it to grief, and some of it was, but it was also the trauma of witnessing my brother's death.

When Marco was killed, the story my parents told to the world was he had died in a mugging gone wrong. My mom explained that two masked men had attacked my dad while trying to steal money from him. She had lied, but I had no idea why and was too heartbroken to argue.

My mom and sisters cried—even Maria, and she never cried—but I couldn't.

I was defective.

Instead, I withdrew into my art. I painted dark abstracts and broken people for hours on end.

While I painted, my mind would wander. I'd try to decide

if I could have done anything differently to help. I debated why my mom and dad would lie and how my dad could fight like the action heroes on TV. I contemplated why my father would have left Marco behind.

The answers weren't quick to come, but over time, I put the pieces together.

As I grew up, I watched my family with a critical eye. They never figured out I knew, but I did. I knew about everything. Every secret. Every lie. Our entire family tree was built on them. How do you learn to trust the people closest to you when they look you in the eyes and lie to your face?

Lie after lie.

Never truth.

The one place there was any honesty was in my studio. In my art.

That was where I found myself the day after my luncheon fiasco with my mother—allowing my emotions to bleed out onto the canvas. Sometimes, I had a specific image in mind when I began to paint, and sometimes, I started a painting without the slightest clue of where the brushes would take me.

Tonight was one of those nights.

The painting had started as a portrait of a young woman, but strokes of yellow and green wound their way around her, snakes curving around her upper arm and into her wavy hair. Her eyes held a sadness, but she wasn't afraid. The snakes weren't her enemies; they were a part of her.

"Your work is remarkable, always has been." My dad's rumbling voice filled the room, and I glanced back in greeting.

Considering his occupation, he could seem surprisingly

ordinary. He looked like any other middle-aged man, well dressed and fit. He was attractive but otherwise average to the unsophisticated eye. I was always torn on my feelings toward him. I respected that he'd taken down the men who killed my brother, but if it hadn't been for his choices in life, my brother would have likely still been alive. Because of that, I'd never been able to get close to him. However, the older I got, the more leeway I gave him because I realized that my genes had come directly from him, and I was no better.

"Thanks, Dad. You need something?" I asked, setting down my brush. I cut right to the chase because I wasn't interested in company. My mood had remained decidedly dark since the day before.

"Not really. I wanted to thank you for indulging your mother with the party. You know how much she loves her parties."

"Yeah, I know, even if she is meddling where she has no business," I griped, eyes on my fidgeting hands.

"Try to remember there are two sides to every story."

Is that what you'd say if I invited your enemies over for tea? I desperately wanted to ask but kept my lips tightly sealed. He knew I wanted nothing to do with Nico, yet he still supported my mother in her plotting. "I'm an adult, Dad. I don't need either of you trying to arrange happy reunions on my behalf." The words were clipped as I glared at my father.

He pursed his lips and lifted his chin. "I'm afraid it's a little late. When your mother told me she'd run into Nico, I suggested she invite him for dinner."

"Just cancel. Things come up all the time. Tell him we have an illness in the family."

Dad raised his brows, then cast his gaze toward the hallway.

"*Tonight?* He's here *now?*" I spat incredulously.

He gave a tight, apologetic smile.

I couldn't believe this was happening. Surely, my mom could tell after our painfully awkward lunch that pushing the issue wouldn't be a good idea. Surely, she had more common sense than that.

Yet judging from my father's grimace, the answer was no. No, she didn't.

"No problem," I said, turning back to my canvas, ears hot with anger. "You guys enjoy your dinner."

"Sofia," Dad warned coolly.

"I'm not a kid anymore. You can't make me do something I don't want to do."

"You may be an adult, but that doesn't excuse you from being rude. Members of this family do not hide in their rooms when we have a guest." His tone was absolute. He was not going to budge on the subject.

I didn't want to start my stay with my parents bogging us all down in an ugly fight. After years of practice biting my tongue, I could put the skill to use, then make damn sure my parents understood this was never, ever to happen again. "Fine. I'll be there in a few minutes." Though the words were a concession, nothing was conciliatory about my tone. I wanted there to be no misunderstanding that I was not happy about this.

"Good girl," he murmured, reaching out to stroke my hair. "You know we only want what's best for you." He gave one more tight smile, then left the room.

Once I was alone, my lungs deflated, and my shoulders

curved inward. In less than twenty-four hours, I was being forced to face Nico for a second time. At least I had a moment to compose myself before our next exchange.

I grabbed my phone to go clean up and noticed a text from Michael.

You surviving your family?

I huffed out a laugh at the accuracy of his question. That was what I did when I was with my family—survived. I was never happy. I just drifted from one day to the next.

I suppose. If I need to be rescued, I'll let you know. *Rescued. Why should I need to be rescued from my own family?* I wasn't a child anymore. Didn't I have the strength to take control of my life rather than let them lead me along like a trained retriever?

Lunch tomorrow?

I'm helping my mom get ready for graduation. Next week?

Sounds good.

The more I thought about it, the more determined I became. If my parents insisted I joined them for dinner, then I would do it on my terms. Hell, if I truly wanted, I didn't have to stay at their house. Not everything in life was a choice, but I had to take ownership of the things under my control. It was easy to bitch and moan about things just because they were hard, but that didn't mean there wasn't a choice. Sometimes, circumstances made that choice a difficult one, but it was still a choice.

Dinner was my choice. I would attend my parents' little setup, but I wouldn't play the simpering, wounded puppy. I would be the strong, independent woman I knew myself to be. Nico could only upset me as much as I allowed him to, and I was choosing not to let him affect me at all.

I was a Genovese, and we were made of cold steel.

Being home had allowed me to regress and fall into being the scared little girl I'd been for so long. In a matter of hours, I'd forgotten the woman I'd become. They didn't know that side of me, but they didn't know a lot of things. It was no surprise Michael was the one to remind me, even if that hadn't been his intention.

Michael had been my lifeline after Nico left. He picked me up off the ground, dusted me off, and helped me find myself.

In my family, we all had secrets, and Michael was mine.

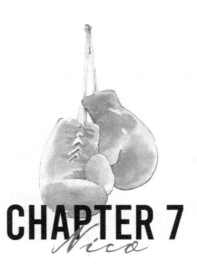

CHAPTER 7
Nico

NOW

The house smelled like minestrone, just as I remembered. I didn't spend a ton of time at her place when we were younger, especially when puberty hit and her dad got more protective. Most of our time together was spent at school, but I did visit her house on occasion, and the place often smelled like minestrone.

I had mixed emotions about being there. Part of me dreaded the stifling awkwardness of sitting near her and knowing she hated me. I hadn't had a particular plan going into our little lunch setup, but I still managed to surprise myself at how I handled the situation. I had needed to ease tensions and get her to let me in, but I hadn't intended to cut myself open for her. The words fell from my mouth before I could stop them. When I saw her look at me with such raw pain, I couldn't help myself. I had needed her to know she wasn't alone.

My sentiment wasn't exactly well received.

At least our initial reunion was over—I had known it would be the hardest part. Dinner might turn out to be just as much a cluster fuck as lunch had been, but part of me didn't care. Part of me would still rather get to see her, touch her, smell her, than leave her in peace.

Yeah, I was an asshole.

Of course, when Enzo suggested I stopped by for dinner, it wasn't like I could refuse. If I'd had a choice, would I have taken it? Probably not. I wasn't the playground protector Sofia had grown up with. The boy she'd known grew into a hardened, selfish man. There was a time I would have done anything to keep her from being upset, but now, I'd spent too many years looking out for my own best interests. After feeling my lips on her skin, smelling the berries and cream scent on her hair, and seeing the flecks in her hazel eyes, I wanted more—whether it hurt her or not.

When Mrs. Genovese directed me to the dining room, I noted that the wallpaper had been changed, but everything else had remained the same. A long cherry red table with eight chairs filled the room, and a formal china cabinet loaded with breakables lined the back wall. Four places had been set on one end—the head of the table, one on the near side, and two on the far side. The two seats together were clearly intended for us, and I wondered how Sofia would respond.

"So, Nico, Enzo tells me you're quite the professional boxer." Carlotta looked at me expectantly even though she hadn't technically asked me a question.

"Yes, ma'am. It's harder to find competition in the heavy-weight division, so I don't fight all that often anymore."

"I'll bet. You ended up growing so much since we saw you last! How tall are you now?"

"Six four. The last four inches didn't hit me until my twenties."

"Isn't that something? Of course, you were always big for your age, but still ... I almost didn't recognize you!" We both gave a small laugh just as Enzo joined us at the table. Mrs. Genovese poured some wine, and we visited about inconsequential matters as we waited for Sofia to join us. All the awkward small talk had been worth it the moment she stepped into the room.

Hair pulled up in a twist, Sofia stepped gracefully into the dining room in a vibrant red dress that clung to her lithe frame, accentuating her modest curves. She wore a broad smile painted blood red to match her dress. She was sexy as fuck, and my dick stirred to life just at the sight of her.

This was not the same woman I had encountered the day before.

Sofia had come to dinner ready to play, and I was more than game. Her reaction at lunch had been raw and honest; this was a show ... a challenge.

I lived for a good challenge.

"Sorry to keep you all waiting. I had to freshen up." She walked without hesitation to the seat next to me as I stood to help her into her chair. "Thank you, Nico."

"My pleasure," I responded, my voice a sensual caress.

She pretended to be unaffected, but the hairs along her arms stood in response to my voice. I fucking loved it. Sofia and I never had the opportunity to fully explore each other sexually, and it was clear I had missed out. We were so in tune with one another that her body couldn't help but respond to mine. Sex with her would be worth the one-way ticket to hell I would earn, if I wasn't headed there already.

The room suddenly heated from the influx of sexual tension, along with her parents' understandable discomfort.

"Well," called out Mrs. Genovese. "I suppose I'll grab the antipasti." She scurried off to the kitchen, quickly returning with a platter of meats and cheeses.

"Mom, everything smells delicious," said Sofia as she reached for her glass. "I'd say this evening calls for a toast."

We each lifted our glasses, and Enzo narrowed his eyes at his daughter, just as aware of her games as I was.

"To long-lost friends and unexpected reunions." She cut her eyes over to me, a saccharine smile on her lips.

What I wouldn't have given to see those lips swollen and smudged after I'd kissed her senseless. She thought she was running the show—that she could sweep in here, toy with me to her amusement, and then walk away without a backward glance.

She didn't have any clue who she was dealing with.

Before we brought our glasses down to drink, I added my own contribution. "To new beginnings and to *happy endings*." I laced my toast with a heavy dose of innuendo, holding her gaze captive as I said the words. There was a good chance Enzo was going to jump up and rip my throat out for the comment, but I'd needed to show her she couldn't affect me.

Her throat bobbed as she struggled to swallow while we clinked glasses. She then cleared her throat and brought her glass to her mouth. I was envious of the deep red liquid as it touched those lips, and I wondered if the wine would make her even more brazen or send her crawling back into her shell.

Enzo and Carlotta began to serve themselves, but the moment I lifted my hand to reach for the platter, Sofia sat tall.

"Please, let me. You're not big on cheese, as I recall, so some of the meat and maybe an olive?" She placed a few items on my plate, accidentally sending one of the olives onto the table. "Oops! Guess this one's mine." She picked up the olive and placed it between her lips, sucking gently at the juices and holding my gaze before the olive disappeared into her mouth. "Mmmmm ... tasty," she purred.

"Jesus Christ," muttered Enzo. There was no way in hell he would be putting up with our behavior if he hadn't been the one to initiate our gathering. He had wanted Sofia and me to connect, so he had little choice in the matter.

Hoping to keep my boss from ripping my throat out, I cleared my throat. "Mrs. Genovese, how are the plans for the big party coming along?"

More than happy to carry the conversation and give us all a reprieve from the tension, Carlotta ran through all the details of the gala she had planned. We ate soup with delicious crusty bread and sipped wine while we discussed the current state of the New York political scene and how far the Patriots would go in the playoffs.

All the while, Sofia and I waged a silent war—a casual touch of her hand on mine in conversation, my arm draped over the back of her chair, her licking the cream from her fingers as she sampled the tiramisu, and my knee accidentally resting against hers as I turned to listen to her father. It was a war between two grown adults where the strikes were strategic acts of casual flirtation, and a direct hit resulted in flushed cheeks and shortness of breath.

I found the whole thing endlessly entertaining because no

matter the outcome, I would win. She was attempting to make a statement about her indifference, but she only succeeded in proving the opposite.

Sofia Genovese was just as much mine today as she was the day I walked away.

And if there'd been any doubt, she had been the one to hand over the evidence to annihilate those doubts, although not by choice. In one of her many sensual parries, she released her long, golden hair, shaking free the strands from their sleek twist. In doing so, she pulled free the necklace that had been concealed underneath the neckline of her dress.

My eyes were immediately drawn to the small pendant in the shape of the Eiffel Tower, and all humor evaporated. My posture stiffened, and she was instantly aware of my sudden change. When she realized where my eyes were fixed, her hand flew to her chest and tucked the pendant back in its hiding place. She made every effort to appear casual and unaffected, but the pulse point at her neck was fluttering like the wings of a hummingbird.

A melee of emotions suddenly raged inside me.

Sofia had feelings for me—after all, hate was a feeling—and she was clearly affected by me sexually, which had given me hope that I might wear down her defenses. But spotting that necklace gave me reason to believe that I was far closer to obtaining my prize than I had ever thought possible. I was stunned she still owned the thing, let alone wore it.

Sofia might not know it, but she was mine.

Now, I just had to prove it.

CHAPTER 8
Sofia

NOW

For days after dinner with Nico, I berated myself for revealing the necklace. I'd been so rushed with my little plan to flaunt myself that I'd completely forgotten I was wearing it. The smug bastard probably left the house convinced I still harbored some unrequited affection for him when that couldn't have been further from the truth. I just happened to like the necklace. It had nothing to do with the man who had given it to me.

I wasn't some love-sick teen clinging to the vestiges of my first love.

That was absurd.

I was a student of the arts, so I appreciated the cultural significance of Paris in the art world. The Eiffel Tower was merely representative of my love for painting. That was it.

How many times would I have to reiterate that argument to believe it?

The thoughts had cycled through my mind so many times it was dizzying. They were there all during Sunday dinner at my parents' house when Alessia brought her new boyfriend, Luca. They'd been present at my first week at work and had been front and center as I accepted my degree today in front of hundreds of spectators. A day that should have been about my accomplishments and the thrill of future endeavors was bogged down by the looming shadows of the past like a nest of gnats I couldn't escape.

Despite the distraction, the ceremony had gone smoothly. I was incredibly proud of what I'd accomplished and the fact that I'd pursued my passion despite the multitude of people who warned me repeatedly about the unemployability of an art degree. Time after time, I had disregarded their proffered advice and stuck to my guns.

I was thrilled to be taking the art world into the twenty-first century by bringing art sales and appreciation into the world of social media. I wanted to market myself to art lovers and foster relationships with people who followed my work, rather than rely on an arm's length transaction through a gallery. I was confident a new era of cultural expansion was waiting to be explored, and I was happy to lead the charge. Until my new business venture took root, I still planned to work in the gallery, but my long-term goal was online sales.

I had my degree and the opportunity to pursue my dreams, so I should have been on cloud nine. I wanted to be. Truly, I had tried. If it hadn't been for those damn thoughts of Nico and the necklace, it would have been a perfect afternoon.

By the time the ceremony was over and we had returned to my parents' house for a private post-graduation celebration, I was physically sick of my own thoughts. Day after day of running on the hamster wheel, and I was no closer to knowing how to handle Nico. I would see him at my party the next night and desperately needed a strategy.

My parents and sisters toasted to my accomplishments with champagne, and we all wore smiles and talked about the upcoming party. I tried my best to participate, but the moment the opportunity arose, I slipped out onto the patio overlooking the bay where the crisp evening air could clear my head.

You don't just cross my mind; you live in it.

What the hell was he thinking to say that to me? Nico had no right to show up out of the blue and drop a bomb like that. Each time my mind replayed his sultry voice saying those words, my blood warmed me from the inside out like the heated fibers in an electric blanket.

I told myself the heat he stirred was purely anger, but I knew deep down it was more. It made me wish I had one more glass of champagne to drown out the thoughts—the ones that whispered what a hypocrite I was. Because as much as I hated liars, I knew I was lying to myself. The heat was somewhat born out of anger, but there was also a much more problematic source. More instinctual. Visceral.

I still craved Antonico Conti.

How could you move on from someone who was your everything? You didn't. That person lived inside you whether they were standing next to you or a thousand miles away. The fact that I still wore his necklace, the one he bought for me, wasn't just evidence that I still cared for him. It was proof that I'd never even tried to move on.

It was no wonder I'd had no other boyfriends. I'd told

myself I wasn't interested or that my studies were my priority, rather than boys. But now, I was having to face that it was all a bunch of bullshit. I had turned my back on that part of my life, hoping it would fix itself and was surprised to check in seven years later and discover the abandoned attic of my love life was the same as I'd left it. A few more cobwebs and a layer of dust, but otherwise no different.

I could have tried to meet someone new, or at least removed the reminders of Nico from my life. And in the alternative, if I wasn't going to pull the weed out by the roots, then I should have owned my feelings and fought for what my heart wanted.

But now, it wasn't so simple.

Now, things had changed.

I had changed, and there was no way I could tell him my secrets.

As I stared at the water's edge, shivering in the cold, I realized that, either way, it had to stop. I couldn't keep holding a torch for him. It was time to let him go or open myself up to him and risk being devastated all over again. Just the thought made my stomach churn violently. Was that my theoretical "gut" speaking, telling me I should walk away? That thought was almost equally as upsetting.

The arguments swirled in an endless whirlpool, getting no closer to any plausible solution. The choppy waters stirred up memories of times when I'd snuck onto that same patio to meet with Nico when he wanted to tell me about his first time driving or how his first day of high school had gone. My dad didn't allow boys over at the house—I wasn't allowed to date until I was sixteen—and no matter how much I argued that

Nico was just a friend, my parents wouldn't budge. He didn't have a cell phone, so we couldn't text. Sometimes, we settled for talking at school or phone conversations, but every now and then, he showed up at my house unannounced and threw pebbles at my bedroom window until I met him outside.

For ten years, from the time I was five until fifteen, Nico was my life. He was good, and pure, and honest. He was my escape from everything I hated about the world. At fifteen, I'd lived more of my life with him than without, and I couldn't fathom ever losing him.

The last year of our friendship, our relationship had started to evolve into something … more—something even more beautiful than it had been before, which I hadn't thought was possible. My freshman year, his sophomore year, we were both in the high school wing of our K-12 private school. It started with sweet notes left in my locker, then progressed to holding my hand in the halls, and on to a first kiss—a stolen moment in the supply closet of the art room.

I always loved Nico, but my freshman year, I fell in love with him.

Not just teenage puppy love. Nico became my favorite part of every day and the thing I pictured in my head each night as I drifted to sleep. He planted himself deep inside the fibers of my being, his roots interwoven with mine like two redwood trees, separate at first sight but one creature when you dug down deep.

When he left me, he'd violently ripped us apart, and my wounds had never healed. I had convinced myself they had—placed bandages over the gaping wounds—but underneath, I was just as raw and damaged as I'd been seven years before.

And now he was back to throw salt in those wounds. Why now? I had no doubt there was a reason behind his sudden appearance. Was I willing to be near him to figure it out, or was self-preservation more important? I wasn't sure what I was going to do, but either way, I was in trouble.

CHAPTER 9

Sofia

THEN

"Can I ask you a question?" Nico asked one day as he sat on the swing next to me.

"Yeah, I guess." I squinted over at him in the bright sunlight. Nico and I had become friends over the prior weeks, and I liked talking to him.

"One of the kids in my class said your brother died. Is that why you've been so sad?"

His question made a thick lump form in my throat. Aside from the night Marco had died, I hadn't cried for him. All it took was one question from Nico, and tears pooled in my eyes. If I said a single word, the heavy droplets would overflow, so I simply nodded.

"Okay. We don't have to talk about it. Let's just see how high we can swing. Sometimes, when the swing is going up and up, I feel like maybe I'm a bird and I can fly. You want to try?"

I nodded again, and we kicked back to start our swings.

That was the one and only time we talked about my brother.

Every day for the rest of kindergarten, Nico played with me at recess. When the end of the year rolled around, most of the kids were thrilled about summer break, but I dreaded my last day of kindergarten. Winter break had been hard enough, and it was only three weeks—but three months away from Nico? I wasn't sure how I'd survive. At six years old, three months sounded like an eternity.

I'd had my sixth birthday back in February. I asked my parents if Nico could come to my party, but they said parties were for family only. That didn't make much sense to me because other kids had friends at their birthday parties, but Daddy insisted. The party was all right. I had hoped turning six would feel different than being five, but it didn't. Marco was still gone, and my heart still hurt for him every single day.

Nico was the only thing that dulled that ache, which was why summer break sounded like the worst kind of punishment. Three months without him. Three months of walking past Marco's closed door every time I went up to my room. Three months without the one person who could make me laugh.

The morning of the last day of school, I dragged my feet until Mama yelled that I was going to make everyone late. It was the last day no matter if I was there or not, but I still didn't want to face it.

Just like every other day, Nico joined me on the swings. I never asked him to, and he never asked if it was okay. He just grabbed the swing next to me and started swinging. Sometimes we talked, sometimes not. Sometimes, we walked around the playground, and other times, we just sat by the big oak tree.

He made me laugh when I thought I'd never laugh again.

"You promise you'll be back when school starts?" I asked him warily when recess was almost over.

"Not sure where else I'd go. Ma says this is the only school I'm gonna go to come hell or high water, whatever that means." He gave me a lopsided grin that made the heavy weight on my chest feel more manageable. "How about this— we'll have a competition. You see how many ladybugs you can find this summer, and I will too. When we get back to school next year, we can see who caught the most. Deal?"

His words reminded me so strongly of Marco's on the night he was killed that I instantly threw my arms around Nico, clinging to him tightly.

He huffed out a laugh, patting my back gently. "Dang, Sof, you're strong for a girl."

"Don't ever leave me, Nico." I whispered the words into his chest, afraid to let go.

His arms tightened around me. "I'm not going anywhere, I promise." The humor was gone from his voice, and I knew that he understood how important this was to me.

When I pulled back, I gave him a shaky smile, then darted inside without a goodbye. There was no reason for goodbye when we would see each other again. Summer wasn't as terrible as I had expected, but I still counted down the days until school started again. On the first day back, I walked anxiously out to the playground. To my amazement, I found Nico already planted on one of the swings, waiting with a wide grin plastered across his face.

"Hey Ladybug Girl, wanna swing?"

And that was all it took. We fell into step as if there'd been no disruption. Each school year, we found every chance we could to see each other, and no matter how much or how little we were together over the summer, we picked up in September as if we hadn't been apart at all.

When I arrived for the first day of junior high, I could tell something was different. Nico was waiting for me at my newly assigned locker. I wasn't even sure how he'd known where it was, but there he stood, leaning against the wall of metal with his arms crossed smugly over his chest.

He'd grown over the summer, even more than he usually did. His T-shirt was snug around his arms, and I had to look up at him more than I ever had before. Something about seeing him there waiting for me made my belly feel weird. Instead of running into his arms like I had every other year, I gave him a shy smile. I'd seen him a few times over the summer, but my dad no longer allowed him over for playdates like he had in the past.

"Hey, Ladybug. Drop your books, and I'll walk you to class," he offered confidently. He took my backpack from me as I worked the combination on my locker, which I had practiced endlessly on back-to-school night.

"You don't have to. I brought my schedule and know where my classes are," I offered absently as I clicked open the door.

"Don't be silly. I want to—that's what guys do for their girlfriends."

I almost dropped my new math book on my foot when his words registered. *Girlfriend? Was I Nico's girlfriend?* I was a girl, and we were friends ... was that all it took? I'd seen my older sisters discuss boys and even caught Maria kissing one once, but I hadn't even thought about any boys that way.

My eyes went wide as I peered up at him, taking in the rich warmth of his deep blue eyes. I could stare into those eyes every day of forever and feel that everything was right with the world. Would I want Nico to kiss me? My heart stuttered in my chest and a tingling warmth spread from my hands up my arms. *Yes.* I would definitely be interested in knowing what it was like to kiss Nico. The rush of thoughts raced through my mind as I stared up at him blankly. Fortunately, I didn't have to say a word.

"I've wanted this for a long time, but we were too young before. Now we're both in junior high, and I want you to be my girl." He nudged my shoulder with his, a small hint of uncertainty slipping through his masculine bravado. "Tell me you'll be my girl, Ladybug." His softly spoken words had a slight rasp, his voice transitioning to something deeper and more masculine.

I wasn't sure what being his girlfriend entailed, but I didn't care. Being Nico's girl was a no-brainer—there was nothing else on this planet I'd want to be. "I'm pretty sure I've always been your girl," I answered back with an awkward smirk.

"Yeah, but I want it to be official. I want everyone here to know that Sofia Genovese belongs to Nico Conti, so there's no doubt in anyone's mind."

"Well, I guess you've got a girlfriend then."

Nico dropped my bag and wrapped his arms around me, lifting me off the ground in a bear hug and spinning us in a circle with a loud whoop. I had a lot of happy days with Nico, but that was one for the highlight reel.

I was Nico Conti's girlfriend.

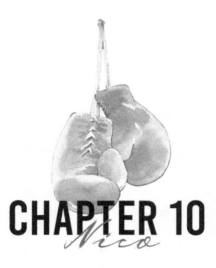

CHAPTER 10

Nico

NOW

I n for a penny, in for a pound—that was what my mom always said. Some things in life were all or nothing, and Sofia was one of those things. The connection that pulsated between us wasn't exactly something that could be turned on and off. My awareness of her was always there like moonlight in the dead of night. Whether it was a brilliant full moon or a new moon only present in the faintest hint of a shadow, it was always there.

Closing my eyes had kept me from having to see her radiance, but now my eyes had been opened. I'd been forced to remember what it was like to have her in my life. There was no way to undo that knowledge. Nor could I walk away before more damage was done.

I'd been ordered to keep her safe, and to do that, I'd need to be close to her. Even if I could protect her from a distance, I couldn't keep her at arm's length any more than I could stop myself from breathing. If I was going to be near her, I'd want all of her. But there would always be so many secrets between us that we were doomed to fail. Starting anything with her was messed up and could only end in a bloody disaster, but I saw no way around it.

The concept of a casual friendship with Sofia was laughable.

Over the years, the longer I abstained from seeing her, the less pronounced the craving, but it was still there in the back of my mind. Now that I'd had a taste, there was no moderating my consumption. I wanted to bury myself inside her—cage her in my arms and never let her go.

That was how I found myself at her house, sitting in the shadows of her back patio like a fucking creeper. I'd told Enzo I was monitoring the place to explain my presence on his security footage. He suggested I come celebrate with them, but I declined. Sofia was likely already suspicious about my sudden reappearance—no need to make it obvious.

I watched her and her family in their grand living room as they toasted to her graduation. She walked through the paces with a mechanical smile on her face, playing the part of the happy graduate. Was it the presence of her family that kept her from enjoying the evening, or was it something more?

She never meshed well with her family. She used to complain about them but avoided the subject when I'd ask her questions. I could understand—my dad and I hadn't spoken in years, and the last thing I wanted to do was think about him, let alone talk to my friends about the asshole. Family was difficult, no matter how you sliced it, and Sofia was never quite like the rest of her family.

I watched them celebrating with no plans of joining in

their little party. For about an hour, I worked through my thoughts, killing time and recklessly indulging in the obsession brewing inside me. My infatuation with her was like a wicked Nor'easter aimed at burying the East Coast in a mountain of snow. I could see it building and knew the effects would be devastating, but there was no stopping it. All I could do was brace for the fallout.

I had figured I'd sit in the shadows and keep my stalker tendencies to myself. However, my little plan was derailed the minute Sofia stepped outside. From the chair I'd planted myself in an hour earlier, I watched as she wrapped her arms around herself and walked to the patio railing. I only caught sight of her profile briefly—a glimpse of her unguarded features in the soft moonlight. To anyone else, she might have simply appeared tired, but it only took one glance for me to know she was utterly lost.

My muscles twitched with the urge to rush from the darkness and steal her away until she recognized that she'd never truly feel at home without me. But just as quickly, I reminded myself why that was such a shit idea, and instead, I continued to watch her and wonder what she might be thinking. Was she remembering the times we'd met out on that same patio years before, or was that the wishful thinking of a man who'd pushed away the only woman he'd ever loved?

I'd never forgive myself for what I did, but it had been necessary.

Protecting Sofia was far more important than my own selfish desires. She was always so innocent, lost in an imaginary world that only an artist could know. It was never my place to tell her about her family—to bring that darkness into her life—and if I'd tried to keep her and my secrets, the inevitable breakup would have been even more catastrophic. I had abandoned that path, and now a detour had rerouted me back down the same dead end. This time, there were no exits or U-turns. I couldn't reverse my way out of this. This time, we would see just how it would play out—every last gory detail.

Unable to hold back any longer, I lifted myself from the cold metal chair. "Just like old times, isn't it?" My voice was a jagged blade slicing through the velvet night sky.

Sofia startled with a gasp, whirling around in alarm. "Nico! What are you doing here? You scared me half to death." In only a few seconds' time, her face displayed a full gamut of emotions—surprise, then fear, before settling on agitation as she lifted her chin and turned back toward the water.

I made my way to the railing, leaving only a few inches between us. "Congratulations," I offered softly—my version of an apology. A part of me wanted to pull her back against my chest and wrap her in my warm arms where she could feel safe, but I knew the gesture would not be appreciated.

A shaky puff of air formed a faint cloud slipping from her lips. "Thanks."

"It's a great accomplishment, but you don't seem all that excited."

"I am. I've just had a lot on my mind." Her eyes cut over to me in a sardonic gesture. "You want to tell me what the hell you're doing here?"

"I wanted to see you."

"Not here tonight. Here as in back in my life. Why now? What's going on?" She turned to lean her hip on the railing, giving me her full attention. I mirrored her stance and took in her delicate features.

Her wavy hair was piled loosely on top of her head, and her flushed cheeks pinked in the cool night air—together, they were a delicious hint at how breathtaking she'd look sated and sprawled in my bed. Not even the cool temperatures could keep me from getting hard after imagining that sight. Hoping she wouldn't look down and see the evidence of my wandering mind, I shrugged my coat off and wrapped it around her narrow shoulders.

"You've been out in the cold for too long. You're going to freeze to death."

"You didn't answer my question."

"I don't have a good answer for you. Your parents reached out, and it started me thinking. One thing led to another, and now you're all I think about."

"You can't keep saying those things," she whispered, her eyes searching mine.

"Why not? It's the truth. That's all I've ever wanted for you—something true, something real." Lies and deceit were all I could give her. I couldn't face myself if I spent every day of our lives lying to her face.

"Reality isn't always pretty."

Didn't I know it. I was surprised at the bite in her words and wondered at what all I'd missed in her life through the years. The thought of someone hurting her made my fists clench with rage. "I'm well aware of just how ugly this world can be. That's exactly why I left."

"Is that your deluded way of saying you were trying to protect me?" she shot back, eyes sparking with anger.

"It's not deluded. I *was* protecting you. I'm not a good man. You deserve far better than I could have given you." My emotions began to get the better of me. I ran my hand through my hair, attempting to calm the spike in my temper.

"That wasn't your call to make." Her finger jabbed against my chest as she spat her words. "Did I ever once give you the impression my love had conditions? Don't you think I know that nobody is perfect? You may not have seen your own light, but to me, you were as bright as the summer sun. When you left me, I drowned in the darkness."

"I had nothing to offer you—" Before I could finish, she cut me off.

"Your love was all I ever wanted," she hissed, her eyes glassy with unshed tears.

We both quieted, our heaving breaths the only sound penetrating the white noise in my brain. Her words had disoriented me. Made me question everything I thought I had known ... everything I'd felt so certain about.

Fuck!

I'd run these same traps before—questioned myself and debated my doubts—and I wasn't going to fall onto that landmine all over again. Not allowing myself time to reconsider, I lowered my shoulder to plant in Sofia's belly and lifted her into the air.

"What the hell are you doing? Nico! Put me down!" She slapped her hands against my back, and I held her flailing legs close to my chest, keeping them secured in place.

I quickly took one hand and placed a resounding slap on her ass cheek. "Stop all that noise before you wake the neighbors." I turned to exit the porch and caught sight of Enzo eyeing us from inside. I held his steely gaze for a long second, wondering if I'd just gotten myself in a shit ton of trouble, but the older man simply turned back toward his wife.

Sofia's shock at me swatting her ass had quieted her during my exchange with Enzo, but the moment I took a step toward the stairs, she resumed her protest. "God help me, if you don't put me down, I'll scream so loud I'll wake more than just the neighbors."

"Anyone ever told you, you're cute when you're pissed?" I asked, smirking as I continued to carry her around the side of the house.

"Nico Conti, I'm *serious*. You can't just steal me from my parents' house."

"Your father saw us. He knows you're with me."

"And I suppose that makes any of this okay? Where are you taking me? This is ridiculous," she groused before slapping my backside.

"Careful, I'm not above retaliation."

"Apparently, there's not much you *aren't* willing to do."

Ah, Sofia. You don't know how right you are.

I opened the passenger door to my car, then set her down. "Get in."

"I'm not going anywhere with you," she said defiantly, arms crossed over her chest.

"Sofia, I'm not going to hurt you. I have an errand to run, and we clearly have things to discuss, so you're coming with me. Now, get in the car."

"How do I know you aren't going to hurt me?"

"Have I ever hurt you?"

Her eyes answered for her. The raw pain in those hazel depths gutted me.

Reaching out, I swept a stray curl from her eyes. "Not what I meant, Ladybug. I'd never lay a hand on you."

Her gaze dropped, and she huffed out a breath before slipping into the passenger seat. "Can't believe I'm doing this," she muttered just before I closed the door.

I smirked as I walked to the driver's side. I was just as surprised as she was, although clearly more optimistic about the unexpected turn of events. Getting a captive audience with her was a tricky prospect, and now she was mine for as long as I needed. Hell if I knew what I would say, but getting her alone was a start.

"I have a brief meeting with someone in Jersey City. I'll bring you back as soon as I'm done," I offered as a small concession, hoping to get her hackles down.

"At ten o'clock on a Friday night?" She paused, her eyes glancing over at me. "What exactly do you do now?"

"I'm a professional boxer. I fight for a living."

The car was silent for several minutes before the feather-light touch of her fingers ghosted over the skin of my knuckles. Or rather, the scar tissue on my knuckles. My skin was mottled and bumpy where it had been busted open and healed over too many times to count. All the joints were thick from injuries and misuse, giving my hands a gnarly appearance.

"What about the piano? Do you still play?" she asked quietly.

"Not really. Mom makes me when I visit her, though."

"Why not? You should. You used to love playing."

I shrugged, not taking my eyes from the road. "I guess I've been too busy for the inspiration to strike me."

Our private school had the option of piano classes for its students. I had been thrilled at the age of six when I started learning to read music. Ma found some rickety old piano for sale so that I could practice at home, and it became one of my favorite escapes. When my world changed, I quit playing because there was no room for it in my new life.

"That's just silly. There's always time to play music." She spoke under her breath, wiping invisible lint from her lap.

I didn't respond. What she said was true, but I had no interest in discussing it.

"How's your mom? She doing okay?" she asked after a brief silence.

"Yeah. After she finally divorced my dad, her life got better. It was a little harder at first, but definitely an improvement in the long run. She moved to Queens and works in a small bakery. I try to help her out, but she's stubborn." I'd have forced the issue if Ma was unhappy, but she enjoyed her independence.

"I guess boxing pays well," she murmured, eyes taking in the premium features of my car. "I never imagined you'd keep fighting. I thought it was some kind of phase or something." She laid her head back against the headrest, her eyes hooded.

Her words took us both back to the day I broke it off between us. There was a heavy silence in the car, so thick with tension I expected the windows to fog at any moment. Neither of us responded, both lost in our own thoughts. I had no fucking clue how to fix what had happened. Talking like civil adults seemed like a good start, but after that was anyone's guess.

After several minutes passed, I glanced over to see Sofia's eyes shut and her lips softly parted in the amber glow of the city lights. The vibrant colors reflecting off the passenger window framed her face, making her look like an image from one of her paintings.

She was absolutely breathtaking—and clearly a bit tipsy.

She'd had several glasses of champagne. Between that and the excitement of the day, she'd succumbed to the lure of sleep. As much as she claimed she didn't trust me, she was comfortable enough to fall asleep in my presence. That bit of information was far more telling than any arguments she could give. I knew it. Her subconscious knew it. Even her body was still victim to the inexplicable connection between us. It was only a matter of time before her heart followed suit.

She was too peaceful to disturb, so I made my way to the meet site and parked the car in the shadows where the lights wouldn't bother her. I hadn't been sure how I was going to explain my errand, so I was relieved she was going to sleep through it.

One of the tasks I'd started to handle as capo was to meet with some of our contacts who kept eyes and ears on the other families. The Outlaws Motorcycle Club had been around forever. We understood the value in maintaining a working relationship with them and several other gangs whereas the old-school mafiosos would have turned up their noses at associating with anyone they considered a thug.

From my experience, the club members varied greatly, meaning some were more tolerable than others. This particular meet was necessary to check in on the Gallo family. After Sal's little setup made us look like we'd put a hit on one of theirs, tension with the Gallos had been through the roof. Inside the family, we used iPhones and weren't worried about wire taps, but communications outside the family were best done in person. If we needed information, it meant a trip across the tracks.

I exited the car as quietly as I could, double-checking that I hadn't disturbed Sofia before walking over to where Preacher and Dutch waited for me. Gabe had brought me along on his last meet to introduce me, and I'd been relieved to find the bikers intelligible, grounded guys as far as I could tell. These situations could be dangerous, so I appreciated having reliable contacts.

The two men stood in their leather cuts leaning against a brick building not far from their bikes. No matter how cold it was outside, you could always count on bikers to display their colors where they could be seen—even if that meant over a jacket or ten different layers. Their culture wasn't for me. I preferred our more understated existence, but I found it intriguing.

"Preacher, Dutch, it's good to see you." I held out my hand as I approached, shaking with Preacher whereas Dutch opted for a casual fist bump.

"What's happenin', Nico?" replied Preacher, the spokesman for the twosome.

"Not much. Wanted to know how things were looking in waste management."

The Five Families each specialized in a distinct field. In some areas, they overlapped, but for the most part, lines were drawn so that boundaries were clear. The Luccianos ruled the construction industry in the city. Early on, the Gallos had cornered the market on concrete, but their main gig was waste management. If you didn't want your dumpsters over-flowing, you needed to play nice with the Gallos.

"It's been quiet; almost unusually so," the older man offered in a gravelly voice that could only be achieved with a lifetime of hard living.

"Any word from the old man?" It was no secret that the

Gallo boss was a lunatic. He'd been quiet in recent months, but his years of erratic behavior kept everyone wary.

"Not a sound."

"What about Sal?"

"He's in the wind. Don't know what hole he's crawled in, but it's deep." He paused for a second, eyes peering around. "Rumor is the Russians are lookin' for him too. Sounds like they ain't too happy with you neither."

"We're aware." I nodded. "Appreciate the information. You hear anything else, you know the drill."

"Always a pleasure doin' business with you fellas."

I could see a smile peeking through his heavy goatee as we shook one more time. As I walked back to the car, my mind was busy calculating the mounting dangers and how to keep Sofia safe. It was a small relief that she would let me near her, but to do a thorough job, I was going to need to stay by her side, and that would not go over well.

When I slid into the driver's seat, Sofia was no longer asleep. What I found turned my stomach in a way I hadn't experienced since my sixteenth birthday.

Sofia sat with her knees pulled tightly to her chest, eyes wide as saucers, and her skin completely drained of blood. She didn't acknowledge me when I got in the car. Her terrified stare was glued to where Preacher and Dutch were mounting their bikes.

"Sof, baby. What's wrong?" I reached over and turned her face toward mine, forcing her gaze to lock with mine.

She panted in small, shallow breaths—she had to be seconds from hyperventilating. Seeing me helped pull her out of whatever nightmare she'd slipped into, which resulted in a flood of emotion. Her eyes darted around my face, and she reached a shaking hand out like she couldn't believe what she was seeing. An instant later, she launched herself at me, lips colliding with mine. She didn't just kiss me, she devoured me, hands pulling me close like I was her last meal and she couldn't get enough.

As much as I wanted to lose myself in her touch, I knew something was horribly wrong, and I needed to address the issue. When her frenzy eased, I delicately pulled myself away, holding her face gently in my palms. "What's going on, Sofia?" I asked softly.

Her eyes drifted shut, and a look of devastating pain crossed her shadowed features. "They killed him ... I just watched, and they killed him."

What the hell is she talking about? I slid my seat back and lifted her into my lap. She settled easily in my arms, nestling her head beneath my chin.

"Ladybug, I need you to explain," I pressed, feeling my frustration growing. It wasn't easy keeping my cool, but right now, helping her was more important than losing my shit. "Who was killed?"

"*Marco.*" The single word held a lifetime of heartbreak.

It was sorrow and remorse weighed down with a heavy dose of longing.

Though I'd only heard mention of him a few times, I knew Sofia's brother was named Marco. Considering her despair, I had no doubt that was who she was referring to. Her brother had been killed when she was little, but I had no idea she'd witnessed it.

"Did you see your brother get killed?" It was a heart-wrenching question to ask, but I needed to know.

She sat utterly motionless as my heart pounded in my ears,

making each second seem to stretch out interminably. Had I not been so hyper focused on her, I might have missed her tiny nod against my chest.

Jesus fucking Christ.

How had I not known? She'd been wrecked as a child after her brother's death, but I had always assumed it was her way of grieving. I had no clue she'd been subjected to the trauma of watching her brother die. I tried to remember how it had happened, but I'd been too young, and the incident was rarely discussed.

Then it hit me—she said *they* killed him.

Had she meant Preacher and Dutch? The kid had died years ago, but it was entirely possible. I hated to push for more information, but I had no choice. I had to know what she'd seen. If she could identify the killers, Enzo needed to know.

Had she been unable to describe them as a child? Surely, Enzo knows she witnessed the incident.

"Sofia, those two men I spoke with … did they kill Marco?"

She gave a small shake of her head. I thought that was all I was going to get from her, but then she spoke in a shaking, childlike voice. "Not them—men like them. Men in vests. Scary men," she whispered. "We'd gone to the movies, and I fell asleep in the car. I woke up and saw Marco get … shot. My dad … he … beat them to death, I think. He thought I was asleep. I never told them. I never told anyone. Watching you with those men—it was just like that night. I woke up in the car and saw you walking over to the two men in vests. It was like I was living that night all over again." She pulled back and peered up at me as tears streamed down her pale cheeks. "I was so scared they would kill you too."

I was floored.

Absolutely stunned.

Not only had she seen the entire thing, but she'd never told a soul. All those years we were so close, and she'd never even told me. I buried the small pang of hurt, knowing her inability to tell me about the incident was more about her own trauma than a testament of her trust in me. My heart shattered for her, splintering into a thousand pieces at the horror she'd had to endure all alone.

"I'm okay, Ladybug," I reassured her, wiping her cheeks dry just as more tears overflowed. "I'm so sorry I scared you. I had no idea."

"Nobody does—and you can't tell them. Promise me, Nico. Promise me you won't tell my dad." Her words were suddenly hurried and urgent, making me wonder what on earth she was afraid of.

"Your parents need to know, Sof. Why would you want to keep that from them?"

Her eyes darted around in panic, and she tried to climb from my lap, but I held her firmly in place. "You don't understand," she pled, wringing her hands.

"Help me understand. Why can't your parents know that you were a witness?"

"Because they'd ask questions, just like you're doing now."

I narrowed my eyes, suspicion tensing the muscles in my neck. "What else don't you want them to know? What secrets have you been keeping?"

Her lips pursed tightly together in staunch refusal to speak.

"Goddammit, Sofia! How do you expect me to stay quiet about something like this unless you give me a good fucking reason?" I lost the tightly held grip I'd had over my emotions. She didn't know just how difficult a position she was putting me in, but that didn't make it any easier.

"Is it not enough that I'm begging you?" she asked quietly, eyes pleading in earnest. When she examined the harsh lines of my face and realized I wouldn't give, she dropped her head back in defeat. "My father is a dangerous man. He doesn't know that I know. If you tell him, it will open a whole can of worms that will change everything."

My lungs ceased all movement. Air lodged itself in my throat, and my stomach roiled as if I'd been on an ocean liner in turbulent seas.

She knew.

Had she always known?

All those years we'd lost because I didn't want her to know —didn't want that darkness to touch her—had it all been for nothing?

Rage like the liquid magma within a volcano surged up from deep inside me, demanding to be freed. It wasn't directed at her, but it was there, nonetheless. Fury at the hand fate had dealt us—at no one and everyone all at once. With steel-infused control, I forced my anger deep down inside to be let out at a later time when it wouldn't fuck up all the progress I'd made with Sofia.

"Okay." It was the only word I could force from my clenched jaw.

She peered up at me through her lashes, a hint of confusion crossing her face as she chewed on her bottom lip. "Thank you, Nico."

Unable to resist her sweetness, I pressed my mouth to her forehead, inhaling her delicious scent, using it to help settle the caged beast inside me. "It's time to get you home." I helped her back into her seat, and I could feel the questions filling up the growing space between us. She had to wonder why I'd gone so distant—why I hadn't asked more questions about her father—but she didn't press for answers. Suddenly, the tables were turned, and I was glad for the quiet.

We made the drive back to Staten Island in total silence. I tried not to delve into the abyss of what-ifs—the infinite number of possible futures we could have had. All I could do was live in the here and now, but even that was a mystery. I was no closer to a solution when we pulled up at her parents' house than I was when we left Jersey.

I walked Sofia to the front door. She didn't have a key with her, so we knocked and were greeted by a stoic Enzo moments after.

"I wondered if you two were coming back tonight," commented Enzo as we stepped inside.

"Sorry, Dad. We had a lot to talk about. I'm really tired now, so I think I'm going to head to bed."

Enzo's curious gaze collided with a brick wall when it landed on me. I had no idea what to tell the man, or not to tell him. Therefore, I schooled my features to an absolute vacuum of emotion. His eyes narrowed just a touch, and his chin lifted as he stepped aside to let me escort Sofia upstairs.

I'd been so caught up in debating how to handle Enzo that I hadn't realized Sofia was taking in our entire exchange. When my eyes finally came to hers, dawning realization dilated her pupils and flared her nostrils. That was when it hit me just how practiced she was at keeping her cards held tightly to her chest. Anyone else who had just connected the dots between her father's mafia affiliation and her ex-boyfriend wouldn't have been able to contain their surprise.

But Sofia ... her reaction was nearly imperceptible.

She turned toward the stairs and hurried up with me close on her heels, which was good because she attempted to slam her bedroom door in my face. Fortunately, I managed to get my foot through the threshold before it could shut and forced my way inside.

"*You work for him, don't you?*" she hissed, chest bobbing with her ragged breaths. "Is that why you left? You chose your career over me?"

"Of course, it wasn't that simple. None of it was my choice. And don't you go acting all self-righteous when you were hoarding secrets of your own like a goddamn squirrel getting ready for winter." I shot back my response in an equally hushed tone, both of us attempting to keep our argument from being overheard.

"Telling you about Marco wouldn't have changed anything," Sofia responded. "And it wasn't my place to tell you about my father."

"Oh, but I should have told you about him? That sounds like quite the double standard."

"Not my father. You should have told me about *you*. You were the one I loved. You should have *trusted* me."

"It had nothing to do with trust and everything to do with protecting you. I told you that already. I wasn't going to drag you into that world."

"But you knew—you knew my father was involved and that I was already neck-deep in the mafia, but you pushed me away anyway. Is that right?" Her eyes blazed, and I could feel solid metal doors closing between us.

"I knew your father was connected, yes."

"So instead of trusting me with the truth, you walked away." With those words, the locks slid shut. Nothing I could say would penetrate.

"I did what I thought was best when backed into a terrible situation at the age of sixteen. If that's something you can't forgive, then there's nothing else to say." I turned my back and walked from the room, my heart hardening to reinforced concrete when her voice never rang out to call me back. We'd both been equally at fault for the way our relationship had unfolded, and if she couldn't see that, there was nothing I could do.

CHAPTER 11

Sofia

THEN

"Three whole months of summer apart, then I'll be in the high school wing and will hardly even see you at school. It sucks." Nico took black paint and wrote out the word "sucks" on his blank canvas. Our art teacher had given us free rein to paint during the last week of school after we had taken our final exam. I was happy for any opportunity I could get to paint, but Nico was only in the class to spend time with me. While I worked on capturing the shimmer of stars in a night sky, he was airing his frustrations about our limited time together.

"We'll find a way to see each other, and there's a slim chance we could have the same lunch period next year." I turned on my stool to face him, unable to hide my smile at his uncharacteristic pout.

"Yeah, right. We'd never be that lucky." Eighth graders

rarely had lunch with the high schoolers, but on the rare occasion when a schedule couldn't be worked out otherwise, it had been known to happen. I was just as skeptical as he was, but I wanted to cheer him up. As the end of school approached, we took turns slipping into bouts of frustration over our circumstances. Today, it would seem, was my turn to cheer on the team.

"Things could be worse. I could be going to boarding school, or your parents could move you to public school." I gave him an encouraging look. When he simply scowled in response, I lifted my long wooden brush and dabbed white paint on the end of his nose. For a heartbeat, we both gaped at each other, stunned at what I'd done. Breaking the trance, I burst out laughing, doubling over in a fit of giggles.

Nico finally gave in, a wide grin spreading across his face. "You think you're pretty funny, don't you?"

"Oh, I know I'm funny."

"If you're so tickled at yourself, you can do the honors of cleaning up your little mess." Shaking his head, he took my wrist and pulled me toward the back of the room. The other students continued painting, ignoring our antics, and our teacher was absorbed in grading exams at the front of the room.

I walked to the large utility sink, but the paper towel dispenser was empty. "Let me grab a new pack of towels."

Nico followed me into the large walk-in supply closet full of a vast array of art supplies. We both scanned the shelves that lined the small room, searching for the paper goods.

"There," I said, pointing at a cardboard box on one of the top shelves.

Nico stepped closer, his eyes falling from the shelf down to where I stood below. The softness I'd brought to his features with my attempt at levity fell away, a determined intensity darkening his cobalt eyes. His body closed in on mine until I could feel his body heat touching me, tempting me. Our gazes stayed locked, and my head swam with nervous anticipation.

He was going to kiss me right there in the art supply closet.

But it didn't matter where we were. I wanted that kiss so badly, we could have been in a bathroom for all I cared. My heart tapped out an erratic rhythm in my throat. My hands suddenly became hot and sweaty, unsure what to do. While his gaze never wavered from my wide eyes, mine kept straying down to his full lips.

It felt like an eternity, when, in reality, his slow descent to bring our lips together only lasted a handful of seconds. Then, the moment I'd envisioned a million times over was finally happening. His warm lips pressed softly against mine. It was our only point of contact, but that one single touch electrified my entire body. My eyes drifted shut as neither of us moved, both lost in the sensation of our first kiss. There was no tongue or movement, just a simple touch, but it made my heart swell with love.

When he pulled back, my face split in a wide grin that matched his own.

"A little something to think of when I'm missing you this summer," he said shyly, digging his hands deep into his pockets awkwardly.

"I'll find a way to see you, I promise."

"Not even the cops could keep me away. Now you go back over to the sink before we get written up, and I'll get the towels down."

I followed his instructions, pulling out a new package of towels from the box he brought over, then removing one from the bundle to wet in the sink. With gentle dabs, I wiped at the white paint still adorning his nose.

"There, all cleaned up." I smiled up at him, noticing his eyes dart to where our teacher was working.

"Looks like we better get back to our table." He gestured with a lift of his chin.

Realizing we were being watched, I spun and hurried back to my stool. Twenty minutes later when the bell rang, I glanced at Nico's canvas. In place of the black lettering, he had painted a large red heart adorned with the black dots of a ladybug.

WE BOTH COUNTED DOWN the days until Nico's sixteenth birthday. We had survived our summers apart and seen each other more at school than we had expected, but we still longed for a time when we could be together whenever we wanted. He didn't live within walking distance, and Staten Island didn't have the same public transportation as they had in the city, so it was hard for us to see each other outside of school. With a driver's license, Nico could visit me anytime he wanted.

When the big day arrived, it started out like any other Wednesday. I rushed through my morning routine, then got to school and hunted down Nico. This time, instead of a morning hug, I greeted him with his birthday present wrapped in shiny green paper. His parents didn't have much money, so he had a crap iPhone 3 that died all the time. I'd saved for months to give him the new iPhone 5 that had just come out and couldn't wait to show him. I thrust the package at him, bouncing in place I was so excited for him to open it.

He shredded the gift wrap in two second flat, his brows drawing together when he saw what was inside. "Sof, I can't accept this. It's too much."

"Antonico Conti, don't even think about refusing my gift. That phone means I can text you anytime I want without having to wonder whether it's you or your phone that's dead when you don't text me back. It's purely selfish, so no arguing." I raised a brow, drawing a smirk from him.

"If I wasn't saving for a car, I would have bought a new one myself. Thank you, Ladybug, I love it." His hand snaked around my neck and pulled my lips to his for a chaste kiss. "Later, when we aren't at school, I'll thank you properly," he purred close to my ear.

My cheeks blazed with warmth. "You coming over later?"

"Ma got off work and is grabbing me at lunch to take me to the DMV since their lines take all day. I'll miss school this afternoon, but I'll come by your place when I'm done—driving by myself."

I grinned up at him, so happy to see the joy on his face. "Confident you'll pass, aren't you?"

"Today is going to be an amazing day. I can feel it."

His optimism was infectious, making me giggle as he planted one more kiss on my cheek. "Alright, birthday boy. I need to get to my locker, but I'll see you after school. Good luck!"

"Thanks, Sof!"

I shook my head as I watched him strut down the hall, saying a little prayer that everything went smoothly with his driver's test. Nico was the best part of my life. I shared everything with him, aside from the fact that my dad was in the mafia. I'd debated over and over whether to tell him about my family but couldn't seem to do it. I hated to mar our relationship with that side of my background. It served no purpose except as an outlet for me to vent, so I allowed the secret to remain in the dark.

At six sharp that evening, Nico showed up at my house grinning ear to ear behind the wheel of his father's twelve-year-old Pontiac Grand Prix. I ran out to meet him, throwing my arms around his neck the second he stepped from the car.

"You did it!" I squealed as he lifted me off my feet.

"I told you I would. Did you doubt me?" he asked, easing me back to the ground.

"No, but I've heard horror stories about the DMV. I was just anxious for you."

"What's going on out here?" My father's voice carried through the front door I'd inadvertently left wide open.

"Nico got his driver's license today!" I announced proudly.

"More reason to stay off the roads," my dad teased.

Nico grabbed my hand, pulling us over to where my father stood. "Mr. Genovese, I know Sofia isn't allowed to date yet, but is there any chance I could take her to Mike's Place for a quick dessert to celebrate?"

I sucked in my breath and peered up at my dad, pleading with all my being.

His lips thinned, and he dropped his chin. "Just a quick dessert, and this is a one-time exception because you two have been friends for so long. Your sisters had to wait until they were sixteen to date, and the same applies to you. Understood?"

I raced up the stairs and wrapped my arms around my father's middle. "Thank you, Daddy!"

"You be safe," he said in return, eyes trained on Nico.

"Thank you, Mr. Genovese. I'll have her back shortly."

We climbed in the car and made the short drive to Mike's. At the front register, Nico surprised me by ordering two slices of chocolate cake to go.

"We aren't staying?"

He smirked with a mischievous glint in his eyes. "I told your dad I'd have you back soon, so we don't have much time, and there's something else I want to do."

Giddy excitement sent an electric buzz to my fingertips. Having the ability to drive ourselves presented an entirely new aspect to our relationship ... one I was interested in exploring.

When we got back in the car, Nico drove us around the corner to the shore where we could park overlooking the rocky beach. The sun was setting off to our right, casting long shadows across the water alternating with neon streaks of copper sunlight. The sight was absolutely gorgeous, and I made note of a painting idea that quickly formed in my head.

"I have something for you," said Nico shyly, drawing me from my distracted thoughts.

"For me? But it's *your* birthday."

"I know, but I want you to have it, and I suck at waiting." He held out a navy velveteen box set on the palm of his hand.

My hand started to shake as I reached out to take the small box from him. "Nico, you're so sweet to me."

"You haven't even looked inside. How do you know it's not just plastic vampire teeth?" he teased gently.

"You could have a dead worm in here, and I'm pretty sure I'd love it."

"Whatever, dork. Just open it."

I bit down on my lip as I pulled the lid back and gasped at the contents. Dangling from a silver chain was an intricate pendant of the Eiffel Tower. It wasn't something fancy with jewels, but it was far more precious than any diamonds would have been. Nico knew how much I loved the art world and how desperately I yearned to go to Paris to see its famous artworks in person.

"Someday, I'm going to show you the world, and this is my promise to you. We'll see it all, Ladybug—Paris, Rome, Valencia—I'll take you to every museum in the world if I can." His words were so earnest and heartfelt, they brought tears to my eyes.

"Thank you, Nico. It's beautiful." I gazed up at him, wanting to smother him in kisses. "But I hope you know that even if we stay right here on Staten Island for the rest of our lives, I'm happy if I'm with you."

He smiled softly. "Here, let me help you get it on." Taking the necklace in his large hands, he opened the clasp and placed the necklace over my head.

When I looked up, Nico was inches away, and the car was suddenly engulfed in a sultry heat. My eyes locked on his, and the world around me disappeared. There was no curfew or glittering ocean, no chocolate cake or school the next day—

there was only Nico and my intense need to express my adoration for him.

His lips crashed down on mine in a kiss that encompassed all the passion and longing between us. We had exchanged tentative kisses before, but nothing so heated and intense. His tongue teased open my lips, and I moaned at the delicious taste of him.

I could spend every minute of every day with his soft lips pressed to mine.

His hand trailed from my face down my shoulder and slowly grazed around the side of my small breast. Gasping, I pulled away and glanced down at his hand, my breaths shallow and shaky. I watched raptly as his thumb came around to cup the small mound, then slowly swiped over my nipple. Even through my shirt and bra, the sensation stole the breath from my lungs.

"Nico," I breathed, unsure what I wanted to say.

"I love you, Ladybug. I don't mean to push you. I just needed one touch, that's it." His voice had grown husky, making the warmth in my belly heat further.

"I love you, too, but … I'm not sure…"

His lips quieted me, soothing the stirrings of anxiety that had begun to dance in the back of my mind. His hand returned to my hair, twining his fingers in my long waves. We kissed for several long minutes, making our first official date one of the best nights of my life.

Nico eventually drove me home, although neither of us ever touched our cake. As I lay in bed that night, I replayed the hour we spent together countless times in my head, a broad smile plastered to my face. I pictured future dates and promised intimacies in my dreams that night, unaware that my imagination would be the only place I would experience those things with Nico.

He never showed at school the next day, or the day after.

It wasn't until four days later that he let me know he was alive.

The same day he shattered my heart.

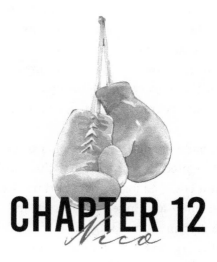

CHAPTER 12
Nico

NOW

I'd never been particularly rash. No doubt that was the assumption when people learned I was a boxer, but it wasn't the case. I'd always prided myself on not being impulsive. My dad was impulsive and undisciplined. He kept our family buried in debt and poised for failure.

I refused to be like my father.

Years ago, when I made the decision to leave Sofia, it wasn't something I took lightly. I wasn't given a lot of time to make the decision, but I took each minute I was given. I carefully weighed my options and attempted to decide based on facts and logic without the muddled haze of emotion blurring my thoughts.

Now, I'd come back full circle and had to decide all over again what to do about Sofia. Did I guard her from a distance and allow her to push me away or try to fix things between us and make a go at a real relationship, despite the dangers it entailed? Circumstances had changed since we were kids, but the situation felt just as difficult to navigate. This time around, I wasn't so convinced it was wise to exclude emotion from the equation. However, if I allowed my feelings to have a vote, it complicated everything. Once you let emotion in the door, it becomes tyrannical and demands full rein of the place. Balance was tricky. I'd gone the route of pure logic before, and it hadn't ended well for either of us. It made sense to do what I wanted this time, rather than what I thought I *should* do, but it could go just as poorly, if not worse.

The uncertainty and indecision pissed me off, even after spending the morning pounding the heavy bag at Joe's. I was almost out of energy and no closer to an answer.

"That bag owe you money?"

I turned to find Tony walking up carrying a gym bag. I hadn't seen him since the night at the bar when I'd had to cover his tab to make up for the jab to the face. Things with guys were so much easier. You fucked up, you bought the guy some drinks, and all was forgiven. Yet nothing on God's green earth would buy my way back into Sofia's good graces.

"I wish it were that simple," I grumbled as I removed the gloves from my hands.

"Nothing like girl trouble to complicate life. I take it things with Sofia haven't been a walk in the park?"

"Maybe if that park was filled with landmines and everyone was decked out in camo."

"Shit, man. What happened?"

I glanced around and closed the distance between us. "She knows about Enzo. She's always known."

His eyes widened in surprise. "How the hell did that happen?"

"Saw her brother get killed and never told anyone."

Tony let out a low whistle. "Jesus. You gonna tell Enzo?"

I ground my teeth tightly together as I took a deep breath. "She made me promise not to."

"*Fuck*."

"Yeah, but it gets better."

"No shit?"

"She figured out I work for him, and now she's furious I didn't tell her."

"She's gotta know you couldn't."

"She doesn't see it that way," I said in a defeated tone. "She's still hurt that I left, even after I tried to explain that I did it to protect her."

Tony's lips thinned. "Well, it *was* rough for her after that. Once you left, that bitch Brooke Britton made her life at school a living hell."

My stomach turned at the implication. "What the hell did she do?"

"Guess she had her eye on you and blamed Sofia for you leaving. Used to pull all kinds of petty shit—nothing major, though."

"Why the fuck are you just telling me this?"

He lifted his hands placatingly. "Easy chief," he said in warning. "You had enough on your plate, in case you forgot." His tone was increasingly defensive as I targeted him with my anger.

"You knew how much I cared about Sofia. You should have told me," I ground out, grabbing my towel off a bench and attempting to cool down my temper.

"It was only a few weeks, then she made some friend who put a stop to it."

I whipped around, taken aback by his words. "Made some friend? Who?" I tried to picture who she might have befriended in my absence but came up empty. She hardly talked to anyone other than me while we were together.

"Some new kid who had transferred at the semester break. I think his name was Mikey or something."

A guy? She befriended a guy when I left?

The image of her saddling up to some other guy, holding his hand through the halls and sharing stolen looks with him made my blood boil with a jealous rage. How close did she get with him? Did he take her virginity?

I had to stop that train of thought before I vomited up whatever I had left in my stomach from breakfast.

I wouldn't have wanted her to suffer while I was gone, but it had never occurred to me that she might run straight into another guy's arms. Was that how it had played out? Had she given any consideration to where I might have been before replacing me, or had her anger at what I'd done given her a clean conscience? When I left, I didn't expect her to join a convent or anything, but I figured it would have taken at least a little time to get over me. Now, I wasn't so sure.

But what about the necklace? Was that a sign she still held feelings for me, or was I a hopeless fool?

The questions were endless, stampeding through my brain and trampling all other thoughts. I turned to Tony, my eyes blazing. "I want to know everything."

LATER THAT AFTERNOON, I found myself back at the Genovese home after receiving a summons from Enzo. I'd had enough time to get my head on straight and was ready to do my job. For now, I would make sure Sofia was safe and play the role of old friend at her graduation party. The only decision I'd made was not to rush into judgment, but that was enough to relieve some of the tension mounting inside me.

Sofia knew I worked for her dad, so I no longer had to worry about explaining my presence. I had time to fix things between us. There was no deadline or time limit to figure out our shit. At some point, I'd have to decide what to do about telling Enzo, but that could wait. For now, I would do my job.

It was easier walking into Sofia's home this time. The bittersweet aftertaste of old memories was still present, but I was prepared for the assault this time. The far end of the hallway was dark—Sofia was doubtless getting ready for her graduation party, but a part of me had hoped to see that pale light signaling her nearness. I shook off the childish longing and focused on what Enzo might need to discuss with me as I followed him into his office.

He gave a tight smile and gestured for me to sit opposite him at the desk. "I thought perhaps you and Sofia were well on your way to working out your differences, but whatever happened last night did not go well. She's hardly spoken today, and if I didn't know better, I'd say she spent the night crying. I don't know exactly what happened when you two broke up, but she isn't going to let it go easily."

The implication of wrongdoing was clear in Enzo's words, and I felt a compelling urge to defend myself. "I did what I had to do to protect her, sir. I wasn't exactly given a choice when I entered this life. Once it was done, I decided not to drag her with me. I did what I believed was best for her." I was relieved to speak up for myself. I just hoped I wasn't opening a door that would get me in trouble.

Enzo steepled his hands, resting the tips of his index fingers against his lips. "You were one of Sal's recruits, if I recall correctly. Am I to understand you didn't want to become a part of this outfit?" His features were totally impassive, giving me zero clue if I was being asked a simple question or providing evidence at my own trial.

"Sal wanted me on board, so he used what leverage he had to coerce me into working for him—to demand my allegiance and become a made man."

"I'll admit I was surprised when I found out you had joined the family. When you were young, and Sofia took such a strong liking to you, I spoke with your father about ensuring you weren't allowed to know about our activities. I didn't want that information getting back to Sofia. I would have preferred she had friends outside the family just to make life easier, but she was so affected after her brother died, I couldn't stop her from befriending you. As you two grew up, I wondered how it would all play out. Last I had heard, you didn't know anything about the family until you were suddenly among our ranks. Then you two broke up, and it was no longer an issue."

"I didn't know anything about the family until Sal and my father gave me a crash course. I happened to see you that night outside the warehouse I'd been taken to. I thought maybe you had been a part of recruiting me—that you had ordered my initiation."

He shook his head, lips pursed. "Unfortunately, no. It was yet another poor decision made by Sal. No one wants a man who doesn't want to be made, but there's no going back. I trust that isn't an issue now?" he asked with a slight lift of his brows.

"That was a lifetime ago. I've made my peace with where I am and made the outfit my family." I infused my gaze with every ounce of confidence and certainty I possessed. I didn't want to give Enzo the slightest shadow of a doubt as to my loyalties.

After an eternal second, he lowered his hands. "You'll need to fix this business with Sofia. She'll be moving out of our house soon, and I want someone guarding her."

"I'm working on it." *Not for the reasons you think.* He wanted me to protect her, and I wanted to get her naked beneath me. The brief kiss we'd shared wouldn't stop replaying in my head, no matter how messed up the situation had been. I wanted more. A hell of a lot more. If I accomplished my mission, did it matter how I did it?

A small voice inside me cleared its throat and insisted this would be the perfect time to tell Enzo that his daughter knew about the family. I'd sworn an oath to the outfit, so I owed this man my absolute loyalty. So why did my lips refuse to budge? The *family* was supposed to outrank our own blood relations. Outrank any and all other obligations. But at the sight of Sofia destroyed in my arms, all other promises shriveled into dust.

Nothing came before my Ladybug.

Even my own life.

Enzo drew me back to the present when he continued to speak. "We have a meet with the Russians tomorrow morning to sort out whatever mess Sal has created. I want you there. Once we get the Russians settled, hopefully we can smooth things over with the Gallos and get our hands on Sal."

"Not a problem. Let me know when and where, and I'll be

there."

He gave a nod, then stood and extended his hand. "This may not have been the life you envisioned, but I'm glad to have you with us. You're a good man, Antonico."

I shook his hand firmly. "Thank you, Don Genovese."

"We still have a few hours until things get underway, but you're welcome to stick around. I wasn't sure if I'd get a chance to visit with you once Carlotta put me to work," he said good-naturedly.

"No problem at all. I have a couple of errands to run, but I'll be back in plenty of time."

I excused myself and made my way back to the car. I had a call I needed to make to an old friend to see what I could dig up on this Mikey kid. I wasn't sure why I was prying into Sofia's past, but something didn't sit right with me. Probably came down to unreasonable jealousy. Chasing down some schoolyard crush of hers wasn't exactly rational.

When it came to Sofia, all logical thought exited the building.

With each passing day and every minute we were apart, I became more and more certain I needed to make her mine. If only there were an easy way to make that happen. In my gut, I knew there was only one possibility, but it had just as much of a chance to work as it did to backfire in my face.

I needed to tell her everything, even if she never talked to me again.

It was a risk—not only because she might push me away, but also because I would be breaking my oath for a second time. My need to have Sofia was going to be the death of me, but calling her mine for however long it lasted would be worth that fiery descent into the bowels of hell.

CHAPTER 13
Sofia

NOW

Last night was such a disaster. If I had to list all the ways the night had gone wrong, I'd be at a loss as to where to begin. Probably the fact that I allowed Nico to whisk me away in the first place. He had hit the nail on the head when he said it was just like old times. Standing on the patio with him made me feel like I'd slipped through a portal to seven years earlier. It stunned me to discover just how comfortable and normal it felt, despite everything that had come between us.

The champagne no doubt played a role in my questionable choices. I could have screamed or put up more of a fight, but I didn't. No matter how much he had hurt me in the past, no matter how wary I was of seeing him again, he was still Nico. I couldn't unlove him if I'd tried, which I hadn't. The most terrifying part was that I didn't think I ever wanted to stop loving Nico. How messed up was that? He was an intrinsic part of me, and cutting him loose would mean eviscerating an integral part of my soul.

I couldn't. I wouldn't.

So where did that leave me?

Bawling my eyes out for the better part of the night, that was where. Some of my turmoil had run far deeper than anything Nico had done. Seeing him replay the worst night of my life had brought back all the oppressive emotions linked to Marco's death. I hurt in ways I'd forgotten a person could hurt.

Then the pendulum would swing the other way, and I'd remember the momentary bliss I'd felt when I'd stolen that kiss from Nico in his car. My lips on his had erased all the other hurt and fear. Being in his arms had brought me more comfort and surety than anything ever had before. But it was as short lived as a rainbow trailing a summer storm. When I witnessed the understanding that passed between Nico and my father, the puzzle pieces slid themselves into place, revealing a crisp image of what had happened so many years ago.

Nico became a member of the mafia, choosing *the family* over me.

He had become a part of my father's outfit and, in turn, walked away from me. He could claim he was protecting me or that he was sworn to secrecy, but every rule had exceptions. It had been his choice to push me away. His choice to join the outfit. His choice to keep those secrets.

Everything was a choice.

Why couldn't he have trusted me with his secret? Did he think I would tell someone and endanger him? Did he not realize I was already in danger, considering my father's associations? Whether I knew about my father or not, Nico had to have known, which meant he knew I was already at risk. So how would pushing me away keep me any safer?

No matter how I examined what happened, none of it made sense. I could only assume there was more he wasn't telling me. It was a safe guess—people always left something unsaid. We were creatures of habit, and our most intrinsic habit was the keeping of secrets.

I had thought my relationship with Nico was different, but why, I didn't know. I'd kept my family's secrets from him, so why wouldn't he keep secrets of his own from me? I wasn't purely good or evil. Neither was he.

Maybe that meant I should have cut him some slack and recognized that his actions might not have been purely malicious. I'd tried not to condemn him unjustly, but the pain of everything that had happened clouded my judgment. He had wounded me too deeply for me to view his actions from an impartial perspective.

Startling me from my thoughts, my mom's approaching footsteps clacked loudly down the hallway. I quickly threw a drape over the canvas I'd been examining and turned to the door.

"Sofia?" she inquired cautiously as she rounded the corner. "How are you doing, sweetie?"

I hadn't spoken to anyone at breakfast and had looked positively atrocious, so it was no wonder she'd come to check on me. "I'm fine. Is it time to start getting ready?"

"Just about." Her lips pulled into a thin smile, her eyes flitting about the room. "You want to talk about whatever happened last night? Your father told me you went out for a bit with Nico." She came and sat on a stool next to my supply table.

I wanted to be angry with her for bringing Nico back into my life, but I had a feeling it would have happened one way or another, regardless of her interference. Instead, I just felt defeated, lowering myself onto the stool beside her. "It's complicated, Mama. Seeing him stirs up so many emotions. Sometimes it's good, but sometimes it hurts so bad I can't breathe."

"The people we love are always the ones who hurt us the most. If we didn't care about them, their actions wouldn't hurt."

"I get that sometimes we hurt people on accident, but if you love a person, why would you intentionally do something you know is going to hurt them?"

"Why does a parent spank a child? Why tell your sister the guy she's dating is an asshole? Sometimes it's easier not to do those things, but we do them *because* we love that person. I'm not Nico, so I can't speak for him, but I would be willing to bet he had a good reason for the things he's done. I've seen the way he looks at you—the way he's always looked at you—and there is no question in my mind that he loves you."

"So, you think good intentions can absolve someone of their wrongdoings?"

"Well, that's a broad statement if I've ever heard one." She arched a brow at me. "It's presumptive to say good intentions are always enough, but sometimes, yes, I think a person's intent can be grounds for forgiveness. We're all just doing the best we can. Maybe you would have done things differently, but that doesn't mean he wasn't doing his best."

For a second, I wondered if our conversation had more

than one meaning. I wasn't sure if I was reading into it because I knew about Dad, or if she was sensitive to Nico's plight because of her own choices in life. Either way, I could see how her words applied to both situations and wondered if it was intentional. "I see what you're saying, but it doesn't make trusting him any easier, and it doesn't erase the pain."

"I know, baby. That's what alcohol is for."

I looked over at her, and we both burst out laughing. How could this woman make me want to strangle her one minute and laugh the next? Was I not entitled to a single simple relationship in my life? Of course, things with Maria were simple. She asked me about school, and I asked her how life was treating her. We both gave vague, meaningless answers and moved on. Simple. And totally worthless.

I sighed, leaning over to give my mom a hug. "Thanks, Mama. I needed that."

"Anything for my baby girl. And I wasn't kidding about the alcohol. How about you go get in the shower, and I'll bring up a glass of wine."

"If you insist."

With a smile, she tapped my nose and left for the kitchen.

An hour and a half later, I wrapped up the finishing touches of my outfit and examined myself in the full-length mirror. The dress was perfection—even more beautiful now than I remembered it being in the store. I had pulled my hair up to make sure the low back and reverse necklace were visible, put in understated diamond stud earrings, and topped off the look with a delicate platinum bracelet. The touch of aquamarine in the necklace gemstones brought out the hazel in my eyes, and the dress gave me the illusion of curves.

I felt seductive in the dress—powerful even.

It was a heady feeling and extremely important when I'd be seeing Nico again. Or at least, I thought I would. In actuality, I had no idea what to expect. He had indicated the ball was in my court, but did that mean he would keep his distance? What if he didn't even show up? The possibility stole a chunk of my newly manufactured confidence like the big bad wolf blowing down the little piggy's straw house.

Oh well, nothing another glass of wine can't fix.

I went to slide my phone into my small black clutch and noticed I had missed a text from Michael.

Sorry I missed seeing you yesterday. Seeing his words made me smile as I typed out my reply.

No problem, it was a busy day. I take it you got my gift? In the morning before my graduation ceremony, I'd stopped by his apartment knowing the rest of the weekend would be crazy busy. He'd given me a key to his place a long time ago, but I rarely used it.

It's perfect, thank you. Ready for your party?

As ready as I'm going to be. Lunch Monday? I wanted to ask him more about the cop but didn't want to do it over text. On Monday the gallery was closed, so I'd have a chance to have a long lunch with him and catch up.

Sounds great.

"Sofia, you look amazing!" Alessia stood just inside my doorway, her hands over her mouth and a look on her face like a mother sending her daughter off to prom.

"Hey, Lessi! How are you?" I threw the phone in my clutch and hurried over to give my big sister a hug. She wore a gorgeous long-sleeve coral gown that hugged her curves like a second skin. Her dark coloring was the perfect accent to the dress—a shade I would have looked dead in.

"You said you found a dress when we talked on Sunday, but you didn't tell me it was so stunning." She pulled back and forced me to take a spin, admiring the total package.

"Well, I was a little more focused on my run-in with Nico at that point."

"I can't believe Mom did that, but she probably had no clue what she was doing. I'm sure she thought she was helping." Alessia had heard through the rumor mill at school about my breakup with Nico, but I'd never given her the ugly details. It had been too painful to discuss with anyone.

"Whatever she was thinking, it didn't end there. They had him over for dinner the next night. He seems to think there's still something between us, but I don't see how it could work." I plopped down on my bed, feeling deflated.

Alessia sat next to me, her face a mix of emotions. "I had the same thoughts when I first met Luca, but sometimes things have a way of working out. No matter what, I'm Team Sofia, so whatever you decide, I'll support it."

"Thanks, Lessi. He's supposed to be here tonight, and I'm nervous about seeing him. We fought last night and said some ugly stuff."

"If he makes you uncomfortable, you give me a sign, like a safe word, and I'll have Luca kick his ass out of the party."

"You haven't seen Nico recently; he's huge."

A mischievous glint lit her eyes. "You haven't seen Luca fight; he's incredible."

"Why exactly have you seen Luca fighting?" I asked with a curious grin.

"Some guys tried to mug me. It's a long story. The point is, I have no doubt he could escort Nico out of here in a heartbeat."

"A kidnapping *and* a mugging? What the hell is going on with you lately?"

"Don't remind me. It's been one hell of a month." She rolled her eyes, then grabbed my hand and pulled us up. "Come on, let's get this show started. And remember, you need assistance, you come find me."

I squeezed her hand. "Thanks, Lessi."

We made our way downstairs to find the formal living area had been transformed into a sophisticated arrangement of glittering white lights, crisp ivory table linens, and decadent Madonna Lilies. The party would be indoor/outdoor, so the décor spilled out onto the patio where glowing heaters stood at regular intervals to keep the spring air from feeling too chilly.

My mother had done a beautiful job. The look was formal but not austere or gaudy—she had achieved an elegant atmosphere for the evening, and I would have to thank her for all her efforts. Just because I preferred not having a party didn't mean I couldn't appreciate what she had done on my behalf.

Family and friends began to arrive in droves as the sun set over the bay. I stayed inside, greeting each of the new guests as they entered. That was how I knew Nico hadn't come. After an hour of receiving, I moved toward the main gathering and snagged the first cocktail I could find. It had been ages since I'd had to do so much small talk at once—probably Mom's Christmas party if I had to guess. It always amazed me how mentally exhausting it was to plaster people with social niceties and exchange meaningless banter.

I threw back my drink, noting I needed to have some food before I made myself sick. When I made my way to the trays of hors d'oeuvres, I found Maria standing stoically against the wall, watching the party as if she were hired security. Granted, she was gorgeous security, but security nonetheless. She had my aunt Vica's classic beauty—strong cheekbones and full lips she accented with bright red lipstick. Her thick, dark hair and rounded curves made her look like a fifties pin-up model where I was more surfer-chic most days.

"Having a good time, I see." My comment was loaded with sarcasm, but that was Maria's preferred method of communication.

"You know I hate weddings," she cringed.

"I hate to break it to you, but this isn't a wedding."

"Might as well be with all the white and the well wishes. It gives me the creeps."

I set a slice of fresh bruschetta on my plate and peered up at her. "You're an odd individual, you know that?"

Her lips pulled back in a wicked grin that would have given Cruella de Vil a run for her money. "You have no idea."

This time it was my turn to give a devious smile. "What I know might surprise you." I didn't wait for a response. I simply winked and wove my way back into the crowd. I had no idea why I'd hinted at what I knew. Maybe I was tired of keeping all the secrets. Our lives always felt like some kind of twisted game of who could keep the most secrets, but now, it was starting to feel empty. Pointless even. I wasn't about to do anything rash, but I enjoyed giving her something to mull over.

As I maneuvered through the throng of people, I sensed the heavy weight of someone's stare following me. Pausing, I subtly scanned the room until my eyes landed on Nico standing against the far wall.

He came.

His sudden appearance affected me far more profoundly than I would have preferred. It was the first time I'd ever seen him in a tuxedo, and the sight had my knees feeling weak. As if he knew his effect on me, the corners of his mouth twitched up, but his gaze never wavered. Like the Pied Piper playing his hypnotic melody to lure lemmings out of the city, Nico's presence commanded me to come closer. Without permission from me, my body obeyed his unspoken orders, and I forged a path through the sea of bodies straight to where he stood.

"I wasn't sure you'd come," I said quietly, my eyes still locked on his.

"I wouldn't have missed it, even if only to see you in this breathtaking dress. I should gut every man here for laying eyes on you." His words were spoken in a husky tone that drew a blush to my cheeks, making me drop my gaze.

"Last night you sounded like you wanted nothing to do with me."

"You must not have been listening. I told you that you were the one who had to decide if you could forgive me. I want nothing more than to get you alone and slip those delicate straps from your shoulders until you're bare before me." His hand came up and traced a feather-light touch down the length of my arm.

Even if I had been able to wear a bra with my dress, it would have been no match for how painfully hard my nipples became at his words. I had to fight from arching my chest forward, begging for his touch. Wrestling for control, I took a shuddering breath and peered up at him. "And what if I can't forgive you? What if every time I look at you, I remember all the heartbreak?"

"Then maybe I'll need to give you new memories—much more fulfilling, pleasurable memories—to replace the old ones." His voice was laden with sensual promise, conjuring all sorts of delicious images in my head.

"And what happens when you decide it's more important to keep me safe than to keep me in your bed? Then what?" The question was barely audible in the chorus of voices filling the room, but Nico was so intently focused on me that we might as well have been alone.

He leaned in, lowering his lips to my ear, making my heart skip and dance in my chest. "I learn from my mistakes, and letting you go was the biggest mistake I've ever made. Let me back in, and I'll die before I leave your side." When he pulled back, his electric blue eyes sparked with intensity.

Emotion seized me, tightening my throat so that all I could do was nod in understanding.

"Sofia! I've hardly seen you all evening. Where have you been hiding?" My cousin Giada threw her arms around me, releasing me from Nico's thrall.

"Hey, G! I've been at the front welcoming people. How have you been?"

"I'm good, but it seems like you're even better. Care to introduce me?" She glanced meaningfully at Nico.

I tried to give her a gracious smile, but the attempt fell short. "Yeah, this is my old friend, Nico Conti."

Her mouth dropped open in exaggerated shock. "The boy you were friends with all those years ago?"

"The one and *only*," Nico said with a raised brow directed at me and a hand held out to Giada. He seemed to be implying something, but his meaning was lost on me.

"Well, Nico, you certainly are all grown up." Giada was by

far the most forward and vivacious of us girls—me and my sisters and Giada's two sisters, Camilla and Valentina. Our two families were close enough growing up that the six of us girls were practically siblings. Camilla and I were the same age but never grew as close as Alessia and Giada. The two of them had been best friends since the day they were born. I had made it my mission to give Giada and her big mouth a wide berth. Valentina was a surprise baby, so she was the youngest of the group and was still finishing up high school. I liked my cousins well enough, but hearing Giada openly flirt with Nico made me want to dropkick her back to Manhattan.

Nico must have sensed my sudden agitation. He casually placed his hand on my lower back in an understated but possessive move, clearly making a statement. "Plenty of milk and good genes, I guess," he responded politely.

"I see," she said with a head bob of understanding, turning back to me. "So, you looking forward to moving into your new place?"

"I can't wait. It'll be my first time to have my own apartment, and I'm more than ready. What about you? What's new in your world?"

"My life is super boring. I'm going to have to figure out how to spice things up." She waggled her brows at us, relieving some of the underlying tension and making me laugh.

"Oh Lord, I don't even want know."

She plastered a look of feigned offense on her face, her hand coming to her chest. "Sofia, I can't imagine what you're implying. You know I'm as pure and wholesome as the newly fallen snow."

"Riiiiight," I teased, slowly nodding my head.

"Actually, this is a great time to work on plans. I've been thinking about throwing together a girls' weekend. Nico, you mind if I borrow her for a minute?"

He chuckled, nodding his consent. "By all means. I don't want to get in the way of a girls' trip."

Giada grabbed my arm, waving at Nico as she tugged me along in search of Alessia. "It was great to see you!" she shot back over her shoulder.

The rest of the night was a blur of conversation and cocktails. The one constant was the invisible thread that tethered me to Nico. I could feel it connecting us at all times—no matter how far apart we were or how engaged I was in conversation—as if his warm hand still rested at the base of my spine, reassuring me of his presence.

When the night drew to a close with only a few stragglers left drawing out their inevitable departure, it became clear I'd missed Nico leaving. Caterers bustled through the room, picking up drink glasses and collecting table linens. My parents attempted to convince a very drunk man and his date to call an Uber, and Alessia was on a sofa with Luca absorbed in an intimate conversation I had no desire to interrupt.

My part was done, and I was exhausted. Slipping my heels from my aching feet, I quietly made my way upstairs. On party nights, all family rooms were closed to help keep uninvited guests from wandering to other parts of the house. My door and all the others upstairs were shut, the hall meekly illuminated by what was left of the downstairs lights.

I opened my door, closing it again behind me, and tossed my shoes toward the closet as I made my way toward the bathroom. Just before my hand reached the light switch, I froze, recognizing the presence of someone behind me. When

I spun around, I found Nico sitting in my vanity chair in the far corner of the room, ensconced in darkness.

"What are you doing up here?" I asked breathlessly, a surge of adrenaline racing through my body.

"Fixing things. I've gone around in circles trying to figure out how to make things right between us, and the only solution I can come up with is to lay it all out there."

"I think the truth is a good place to start." I stepped closer and sat on the bed across from him. I wanted to show him I was ready to listen, but also because my legs began to wobble like a newborn fawn at the prospect of finally, after so many years, hearing the truth of what had happened.

Nico took a deep breath through his nose, punctuating the heavy silence. "On my sixteenth birthday, when I got home from taking you out, your father's underboss, Sal, and my father were waiting for me."

CHAPTER 14
Nico

THEN

I couldn't keep a goofy smile from my face the entire drive home from my first real date with Sofia. I knew we were young, and most adults wouldn't understand, but she was it for me. She was the most generous, down-to-earth girl I knew—the most beautiful, the funniest, and the smartest person I'd ever met. I couldn't imagine how anything could ever come between us. We would share all of our firsts and grow even closer together, just as we had from the time we were little.

I had no idea where my life would take me, but I had no doubt she would be there beside me, wherever that was. Our connection was like gravity—it simply was. You didn't wonder if someday gravity wouldn't be there anymore. It wasn't even in the realm of possibilities, so it wasn't worth thinking about.

Sofia would always be mine, and I would forever be hers.

Now that I had my driver's license, we could be together like a real couple—not just texting and stolen kisses at school. I couldn't wait to take her to the movies and Coney Island, or even just sit in my car so we could have time alone. I knew turning sixteen would be amazing, but the reality was even more invigorating than I had expected.

Of course, we still had school, which was the only reason I drove myself back home rather than cruise the streets, enjoying my newfound freedom. My family didn't have a garage, so I found a spot on the street large enough to parallel park and cautiously maneuvered next to the curb. I walked with a bounce in my step to the front door, which I found unlocked. Inside, my father sat on the sofa with a man I'd seen in passing but didn't know well.

"Nico, we was waitin' for you," my dad called out when I walked in.

A sudden sense of alarm made the hairs on the back of my neck stand at attention. When I was a boy, I'd adored my father—looked up to him in every way—however, as I matured and witnessed all the times he failed to come home or heard him explain that he'd been fired yet again, I started to realize that my dad wasn't worthy of my respect. In fact, he was a worthless piece of shit. If my dad wanted something from me, it wasn't going to be good.

"Got my license today and took Sofia out for a bit," I explained cautiously.

My father's friend stood and ambled closer. "You're becoming quite the man, Nico. What do you weigh now, one eighty, one ninety?" I wasn't sure how he knew me. He was well dressed in a long wool coat and shiny, pristine dress shoes—not the kind of person my father usually hung around. He exuded power, and I wasn't about to piss him off.

"Two hundred, actually." There was no boasting or pride in my voice. If anything, I sounded wary despite my attempt at being impassive.

"Beautiful—you've got the potential to be one hell of a fighter," the man said, nodding approvingly at my father.

They seemed to be on the same page, but I had no idea what they were talking about. "Fighter? What do you mean?"

"This is an amazing opportunity, Nico," my father cut in. "This will put you on the fast track to being a made man." His eyes shone with hope and excitement, but I was stuck on the word *fighter*.

"You want me to learn to fight?" I asked, my hand rubbing the back of my neck.

"You're old enough now to know how things work," said my dad. "This city is run by important men, and Sal here is one of them. You won't see his name in the papers, but he controls a fifth of the entire city."

"Like a politician?" I glanced at Sal and confirmed that he definitely had the look of a politician.

"Not exactly, but close," cut in Sal. "I'm a part of La Cosa Nostra—this thing of ours. Your father is also a part of our organization, and he thinks you would be a great asset to us."

Dawning realization struck me, rooting me in place. "You're talking about the mafia, aren't you? Like John Gotti and the Godfather?"

Holy shit. I had a mob boss in my living room, and he wanted me to join them?

Nausea roiled through my stomach, making saliva pool in my mouth.

"It's not like you see on TV." Sal chuckled. "We keep things very quiet now. We're businessmen, just like any other in the city. I'm in the business of making money, and I make a lot of it." He grew more serious, giving a hint at the true gravity of our conversation.

"What do you want me for?" I asked Sal, ignoring my father entirely. He was the one who brought this shit to our doorstep, and it was the final straw. After this little stunt, I didn't care if I ever saw his face again.

"We'd love to have you join our ranks. There could be a lot of money in it for you."

Glancing at my father, I realized Sal was speaking on behalf of him and my father. "You a member of his organization?" I asked, eyes boring into my father.

"I am," he responded proudly. "It wasn't something I could talk about before, but now you're old enough."

I had to fight the urge to spit in his face. The man disgusted me.

I turned back to Sal and his proposition that I join their outfit. "And if I don't want to?" I had to force out the words, terrified of the answer I would receive.

Sal clasped his hands behind his back and dropped his chin to his chest. "That would be unfortunate. You see, your father here has a bit of a problem. He owes the family a good amount of money. With your help, we could even out those scales, but without it ..." He looked up remorsefully at my father, then cast his eyes over to me.

I didn't like Sal for putting me in this position, but that was nothing compared to my feelings for my father.

I hated him.

I hated him more than I ever thought a person could hate

another human being. And the worst part was, I somehow didn't hate him enough to let him suffer the consequences of his own actions. I didn't know exactly what those consequences would be, but Sal made it clear they wouldn't be pleasant.

I wasn't going to tell Sal to fuck off, but that wasn't a testament to some deep-seated love for my father. More than anything, I didn't want to hate myself. As a kid, how do you consciously allow one of your parents to be tortured and possibly killed when you have the power to stop it? I felt weak and pathetic for caving to the pressure, but I couldn't do it. I couldn't be the one who sentenced him to possible death.

"What do you want me to do?" The words were the equivalent of my surrender, my bitter tone reflective of my disdain for what I was being forced to concede.

"You fight for us."

"Like boxing?"

"Exactly."

"But I've never boxed before."

Sal smiled condescendingly. "You're a big boy, and your father here says you're a natural athlete."

My jaw began to ache from the intense pressure of my tightly clenched teeth. How was this happening? How had I gone from one of the best nights of my life to one of the worst? How long would I have to fight? Was there a particular number I needed to reach in order to absolve my father, or would I get sucked in and be forced to remain on their payroll?

Sensing my growing doubts and indecision, Sal drew my attention back to him. "If you can't help make back the money your father owes, we'll have to teach him a lesson—one he may or may not walk away from. You don't want that, do you?"

"When do I start?" I bit out angrily.

"Tonight," he said with a small smile, clearly enjoying his power over me.

I had no words to respond.

I would be fighting tonight—for the fucking mafia. What was I supposed to do? I could see no way around it, so I numbly followed the two men out of my house and into a waiting car.

I should have known their kind of fights wouldn't be legitimate.

I knew jack shit about boxing, but the crowded basement I was ushered into, full of men trading money and the acrid odor of stale beer and piss, was far from a sanctioned facility —even I knew that. My ears rang as I was pulled across the room to a far door. Between the cloud of smoke and low ceilings overhead, I felt like I was suffocating.

Sal and two of his men led us back into a small room where a couple of fighters were getting ready. With a single flick of his wrist, the two men jumped to their feet and hurried from the room.

"Here are some shorts. Get changed and Sammy here can wrap your hands."

I took the athletic shorts from him and began to undress mechanically.

"This short notice wasn't ideal; I'll give you that. After tonight, we'll begin to train you. Next time you fight, it'll be second nature."

I wasn't crazy about the concept of a next time, but if I had to fight again, training so I didn't get my face bashed in sounded good. As soon as I was changed, one of Sal's goons began to weave a long white wrap around my wrists, knuckles, and hands.

"Keep your thumbs here," the man said, placing my thumb outside of my fisted hand. "Otherwise, you'll break 'em when you hit. Make sure you keep your guard up and stay away from the ropes. The guys up front get carried away sometimes and play dirty."

Great, so I was fighting an unknown opponent and an angry mob.

Sal ushered the guy out of the way and took his place in front of me. His face hardened so severely that I wondered if he had a split personality. The Sal I'd been talking to for the past hour was not the same man who stood before me. "The guy you will be fighting against is a fuckin' rat," he growled menacingly. "He spoke with the cops, and a lesson needs to be made." His gray eyes bore into me, squeezing my lungs with their ferocity.

"Are you … telling me to … to kill him?" I choked out.

"Accidents sometimes happen in these matches," he replied without an ounce of emotion.

"I don't think I can do it. I can't just kill someone." Panic began to bubble up inside me, threatening to seize control of my thoughts and actions.

Sal's eyes slid over to where my father stood helplessly watching our exchange. In an instant, one goon grabbed my father's arms and yanked them behind him while the other pounded his meaty fist into my father's face.

"Stop! Please, stop!" I cried out, now utterly terrified.

Sal glanced back at me and narrowed his eyes. "I don't think you get it, kid. I'm not fuckin' around here."

"I get it. I get what you're telling me, but I just don't know if I can do it. I'm just a kid." My words flew from my lips in a single breath—a pointless plea for mercy.

"Then you better dig deep because it's time to grow up. Fast." He glanced back at my father just as one of the men, took my father's arm and broke it in half over his knee. The sickening crunch brought vomit into my throat.

My father wailed a blood-curdling cry, his lower arm flopping unnaturally to the side.

"*What the fuck?*" I hissed, spittle shooting from my mouth, and tears pooling in my eyes. "Why are you doing this? If these guys are so tough, why not just have them fight?" It may not have been smart to question him, but I wasn't exactly thinking clearly—shock and horror had taken control.

Sal stepped closer, pressing his finger into my chest. "Because I want *you*. Now get a fucking grip on yourself before you go out there. This is happening. You may not have expected it, and you may not like it, but none of that matters. Your father's life depends on your actions tonight. Either you pull your head outta your ass and fight like a man or kiss your father goodbye. The choice is yours."

I'd never known evil before in my life, but I had no doubt the man standing before me was the devil himself. He glanced at his men and flicked his head toward the door before walking us back into the main room. One man helped my father through the door, and the other acted as my escort.

The second I appeared in shorts and wrapped hands, the crowd whooped and hollered, ready for blood. The noise was deafening, but I hardly noticed it. I had withdrawn inside my head, watching the scene before me like a movie in my own personal theater. One of the spectators spit at me, and I didn't even flinch.

I was going to have to use my fists to beat a man to death.

The only way I could manage the feat was to go to a place where I was no longer myself. To regress within myself and treat the entire experience like it was happening to someone else.

I climbed into the ring, noting a much smaller man twitching in the opposite corner. He reminded me of a dog I found when I was little. I convinced my mom to let us keep him, so she got a leash on him and we took him to the vet. The thing was so terrified, his tail was tucked all the way beneath him, and he could hardly stand he trembled so bad. The minute the vet touched him, he had pissed himself. My dad had been furious when he got home. The next day, the dog was gone.

I shook my head, doing everything I could to wash the memory from my brain. Nothing about that moment in time was going to help me here. My father was a dick, but I couldn't let him die. I didn't know the other man, so I would do my best to imagine him as a child molester or something as equally heinous.

Someone grabbed my hands and squeezed tiny MMA style gloves on them, rather than standard boxing gloves. I registered the difference but couldn't even summon surprise. Fear, horror, worry, frustration, even disbelief were suspiciously absent. I had somehow severed myself from all emotion, my eyes tracking to where Sal's man stood against a back wall with my father. I vaguely noticed my hand being lifted as the announcer made his introductions, then a mouthpiece was inserted between my lips. The one thing that stood out loud and clear in my mind was the ringing bell that signaled the beginning of the fight.

Tearing my eyes from my father, I turned to face my opponent just as he flew at me, fist hammering me in the face. I stumbled backward, the ref coming between us to allow me time to recover. Men screamed and waved their hands all around us, but they might as well have been images on colorless wallpaper. My hazy state of mental self-preservation slowly morphed into physical self-preservation. It was something altogether more sinister. More aggressive. More deadly.

I hadn't known it was in me, but when fists started flying, something primal emerged.

The stinging pain in my jaw was a wake-up call, but his uppercut to my gut was what flipped my switch. Lowering my stance, I brought my fists up to guard myself and began to study my opponent as he bounced on his toes. The frightened mutt had gone feral when faced with possible death. Unfortunately for him, he wasn't the only one who could transform when properly provoked.

This time, when his fist flew out, I evaded and followed with a hard left cross that got him solid across the jaw. I'd never hit anyone before. The feeling was odd but also surprisingly cathartic. I realized I could take all that emotion I'd tucked deep down inside me and release it onto this man who wanted to hurt me.

It took me a while to get the feel of it, so for five rounds we pounded each other until we were both exhausted. Eventually, the adrenaline began to fade, and the crowd noise filtered back into my consciousness. I glanced to where my father stood to find an angry Sal holding a gun to my father's head. My dad wept openly.

No one else saw.

No one else cared.

But Sal's message was clear. End it, now.

I didn't want to carry the guilt of my father's death. By the end of the night, someone was going to die, and I vowed it would not be me or my father.

Sucking in a deep breath, I turned just in time to block a sucker punch. In response, I rained down a frenzy of blows, catching the man totally off guard. I channeled every ounce of my fury and frustration, pummeling the man into the floor of the ring until he was unrecognizable. Even once he no longer moved, I continued my assault, hoping to put an end to the madness of my sixteenth birthday.

At that moment, I didn't experience a coming of age.

I unleashed a demon from within me that I had not known I possessed.

Eventually, someone dragged me from the man's corpse, and my arm was lifted victoriously into the air. Through my one good eye, I took in the cheering crowd and spotted my father. He was smiling through his tears, his face glowing with pride.

I did this thing for him, but I was disgusted.

I never wanted to see him again because I knew there was no going back.

He did this to me—he put me in this situation.

I had saved his life and damned my own.

I DIDN'T SLEEP at all that night.

I lay in bed, staring at my ceiling, a captive to my thoughts.

I wanted to sleep. I wanted to fall into my dreams and pretend the day before had never happened, but that wasn't to be. I attempted to process what I'd done and what it meant for my life moving forward. I was terrified about going to prison or being killed. I was furious with my father, and even my mom for keeping him around. I was worried about what would be asked of me in the future. But the thing that bothered me the most was the impact on my relationship with Sofia.

How could I possibly bring this shit to her doorstep? I couldn't taint her life with the cloud of evil that now trailed behind me. The boy inside me was eager to suggest we run away together, but that would just condemn her to an equally miserable life. We were kids—she was only fifteen. With no education or resources, we'd be on the streets. It wasn't an option.

So, what did that mean?

An entire night of examining the facts, and it was clear there was only one option for me. I had to let her go. Not just let her go—she'd never simply let me walk away. I had to push her away so she'd never want me back. Life without her would be soul-crushing. Just the thought of hurting her so ruthlessly brought me to tears. I sobbed silently into my pillow, allowing my innocence and heartbreak to drain from me, one tear at a time.

By the time I forced myself from my bed, I felt like hell, but it was no more than I deserved. I showered the crusted blood from my skin, standing under the scalding water until it ran cold. There was no way I could show up at school looking like I did, so I didn't even bother.

When I went downstairs, my father sat at the kitchen table, his one arm in a sling—apparently, he'd been taken to the hospital after the fight. I hadn't cared where the fuck he'd gone, so long as I didn't have to look at him.

He sat working on his spreadsheets for the horse races. Each week, he would research and do numbers, conniving and scheming how to hit it big at the races. Most weeks, he came back emptyhanded and dejected. I didn't know what this turn of events meant for my life long-term, but I'd be damned if it meant I'd turn out like my father.

I went straight for the fridge, intending to ignore his presence, but he wasn't going to allow me that one decency.

"We have a meeting tonight. There are some things you should know before we go."

Without glancing his direction, I pulled out the milk and began to chug straight from the carton.

"You have to understand what it is to be a part of the Lucciano family. There are rules you have to follow. The most important one is Omertá—the oath you'll take tonight."

I had to resist flinging the milk carton against the wall. I knew my ties with Sal weren't over, but it sounded like I was being sworn in, and I had hoped to avoid that. Fucking naïve. My stomach churned, making me regret how much milk I'd downed.

"Omertá is about silence and loyalty. There is no leeway. If you break your oath, it means certain death. You will never, ever speak to anyone about family business—you understand?"

"Do you hear yourself? How could you willingly drag me into this?" I spat at him, disgusted.

"You saw those men. I had no choice," he bit back defensively.

"There's always a choice, Dad. You could have stayed out

of that shit from the beginning or owned up to your punishment rather than making your son take it for you."

He stood, his face growing red. "This is your ma's fault for insisting you go to that pussy school because it's put ideas in your head about how cushy and perfect life could be. Maybe for the top one percent, but for the rest of us, life ain't so pretty. It's time you figured that out. Being a part of the Luccianos is the one shot you got at making somethin' of yourself."

I was a straight A student, an accomplished pianist, and a starter on the varsity basketball team, and my father thought so little of me that he assumed the mafia was my only hope. "Fuck you." I walked away without another glance.

"Meetup is at eight tonight, you ungrateful shit."

I MANAGED a few hours of sleep before the meeting. It was a small miracle because I was increasingly nervous with each passing minute about what would transpire. My father drove us to a small warehouse building that appeared to be used as a distribution center. Inside, a dozen or so men had gathered and conversed casually—some sitting in folding chairs and others leaning against towering boxes.

"Marty, glad you could make it!" welcomed one of the men along with a chorus of other subdued greetings.

"Hey, fellas. This is my son, Nico." He gestured to me with a beaming smile that made me want to break his teeth. Instead, I attempted to be polite as he ran through introductions of names and information I'd never remember. It was important to play my part. I had no other options.

Eventually, Sal showed up and quickly got our meeting underway. "We have a new man to bring into the fold tonight; a man I'd proudly call family. The Lucciano outfit is the finest, most honorable outfit in this city. I knew the moment I laid eyes on this young man months ago that he was meant to be one of us." His eyes gleamed at the surprise that registered on my face.

Months ago? How long had they been considering this little exchange of debts? Or had that merely been an excuse to drag me in? My thoughts were dashed away when the gleam of a knife caught my eye, and adrenaline shot tiny flames through my veins.

"Our family is steeped in tradition, and one of the most important is the oath each of us takes." He pulled out a photo from his breast pocket, holding it up for all to see. "I have here the image of Saint Alphonsus, patron saint of confessions. Nico, come here and hold out your hand."

I stepped forward, eyeing him warily. The room was unnaturally silent, as if even the resident rats didn't dare interrupt this man. Using the blade to nick my palm, he drew a small amount of blood, then squeezed it onto the photo.

"Nico Conti, you have drawn blood for this family, and now your blood has been drawn by the family as we take you in as one of our own. As a Lucciano, you will hold the outfit above all else, surrendering your life and the lives of your loved ones should you endanger the outfit in any way. Do you understand and freely give your loyalty to the family?"

This was it.

There was no going back if I did this.

I could feel the oppressive weight of each man's stare bearing down on me. I had no options. "I do." Two simple words, often the two words spoken on the happiest day of people's lives, but to me, they were a lifetime sentence to hell.

Sal's lips pulled back into a wide grin. He set down the knife and pulled out a lighter, holding the flame to the corner of the photo. "This greedy flame symbolizes the annihilation of all traitors who seek to harm our organization, from outside, or within. When someone takes from the Luccianos, we will take from them tenfold without mercy or regret." His soulless eyes bore into me as he allowed the photo to drop from his fingers and burn into ash on the concrete floor.

The other men cheered and clapped, seemingly unaware of the silent conversation passing between their leader and the newest member. I was quickly swept up in hugs and congratulations, forcing me to smile and play the part of a happy recruit. One of the men informed me that I would start working with him each day to train for my fights. They only laughed when I asked about school, informing me that it was no longer necessary and patting me on the back as if they had told me I'd won the lottery.

When things settled, I excused myself to the bathroom—a tiny, single-toilet room in the far corner of the building. The moment I locked the door, I swung toward the toilet and vomited up the contents of my stomach. Over and over, my gut heaved until only bile could be forced out.

The fight, forcing me into the mafia, denying me the right to finish school—it was all too much.

But there was a room full of grown men out there expecting me to act more than my sixteen years, so I rinsed my mouth in the filthy pedestal sink and took several deep breaths. I needed to pull myself together and go back out there.

I had been in too much of a hurry to turn on the light, so when I glanced to my side at the small window, I could see easily into the darkness outside. There, beneath a streetlamp in the rocky parking lot, was Sal, shaking hands with Enzo Genovese.

An icy chill engulfed my body.

Who exactly was he in all of this? I detected a clear undertone of superiority coming from Enzo. If I had to bet, I would have said that Enzo outranked Sal. If Sal was the underboss, that could only mean that Enzo Genovese was the boss of the Lucciano crime family.

Holy shit.

Did Sofia know about her father? No, I couldn't imagine she did. We told each other everything. There's no way she would have left that out after all these years. I wasn't sure how he'd done it, but Enzo had kept his children in the dark.

For a moment, I wondered if that meant there was hope for us. If he'd kept the two lives separate, maybe I could too. Then images of the man I'd beaten surfaced in my mind and dashed away that hope. I couldn't do it. I couldn't put her in that kind of danger. I couldn't sit across the kitchen table from her day after day and lie to her face. I wasn't allowed to tell her the truth, nor did I want to.

The evening had only solidified in my mind the conclusion I'd come to the night before.

I had to walk away.

CHAPTER 15
Sofia

NOW

I'd told myself for years that no excuse was valid enough to justify what Nico had done to me. No matter what he had been facing or whatever had happened, there had been a better way to handle the situation. After hearing him finally fill in all the blanks from that night seven years before, I began to doubt that conviction.

My gentle giant—I couldn't fathom what it took for him to kill a man with his bare fists. He was the boy who had been sensitive enough to spend day after day drawing a trauma-tized girl out of her shell. He was the boy who texted me about new piano pieces he had mastered. He was the boy who had given me a pendant of the Eiffel Tower with the promise of seeing the world.

He wasn't a killer.

Or at least, he hadn't been.

One glance at his gnarled and scarred knuckles told me

he'd been living in a world of violence since pushing me away. He'd said he was a boxer, but just how much deadly violence had those hands known outside the boxing ring?

My body began to tremble at the possibility of my family playing a role in his suffering. What horrors had he seen in the past seven years? Silent tears slipped from the corners of my eyes. I thought no excuse would be enough, but I was wrong. My heart broke once before because of Nico. Now, it broke all over again *for* him.

"Don't look at me with your pity," he snapped. "That was years ago, and I'm not that same kid anymore."

"I can see that, but it doesn't make it any better."

He unfolded from his chair and reached out to take my hand, bringing me to my feet. "The reason I told you all that was not so you'd feel sorry for me, but so that you'd understand—so you'd give me a chance. You were supposed to be mine. You've always been mine. I pushed you away for a reason, and it was the hardest thing I've ever done. Killing that man was hard, but the pain was over and forgotten in no time. The hurt I caused you burned so deep, the pain has never stopped. But it was the only way I could think of to keep you safe—to keep the ugliness of my life from touching you."

How many times had I dreamed of hearing those words come from him? Wished he would reappear and tell me it had all been a mistake. Nico had been my everything—the only future I ever envisioned. Even after he left, I couldn't seem to picture myself with anyone else, which was why I'd never dated. I had been adrift, clinging to a buoy, but it was land that I needed. Nico was the solid ground that kept my life from falling into chaos. Just having him near me, even though a current of secrets still existed between us, made me feel more at peace.

His hand came up to cup my cheek, his thumb tracing my cheekbone. "Say something, Ladybug. Tell me you'll give me another chance."

"I have some questions," I said hesitantly. "If you knew who my father was, and you knew my life was already tainted by him, why did you do it? Why try to protect me from something I was already entrenched in?" It was one of the pieces to his puzzle that wasn't clicking into place.

"I only happened to learn your dad was involved on accident, and I didn't know until later that he was the boss. What I knew right away—or *thought* I knew—was that you had no idea. I believed that you never would have kept something so huge from me, which meant you didn't know." His eyes hardened as he spoke, clearly still upset at learning the truth. "Your father had tried to give you the option of a crime-free life, so who was I to drag you back in? Even if I did stay with you, was I supposed to lie to your face every day about what I did and who I was? I was trying to do what was best for you. I was trying to put your future before my happiness. I couldn't think of anything more selfish than keeping you for myself despite the dark turn my life had taken."

"But you came back," I said on a breath. "Why? Why now after so many years?"

His lips thinned as he turned, running his hand through his thick hair. "A lot's been going on lately, making our lives more dangerous than usual."

"Does it have something to do with Alessia's mysterious kidnapping?"

He glanced back at me, his face grave. "Yes. Your father has been worried about your safety. Sal Amato betrayed him and did some shit that got a lot of people mad at the family. Sal's still on the loose, and we have a number of dangerous people angry with us."

I had been told Uncle Sal and my father had a falling out, but I didn't know what the cause had been. I was stunned that he would betray my father. He wasn't just a part of *the* family, he was also a part of *my* family. But then, I'd always thought something was off about him. As I grew up, I decided it was just because he was a little smarmy with his child bride and over-the-top flattery. The more I thought about it, the more I wondered how I hadn't seen it coming.

"And how do you play into all this?"

"Your dad wanted someone near you to keep you safe. He figured bringing someone in from your past would be the best way to keep you protected without making you suspicious."

"So you only came back to act as my bodyguard?" My stomach churned as I recalled his claims of missing me—telling me that he never stopped thinking about me. Had it all been a rouse?

"Stop!" he commanded, closing the distance between us and seizing my face in his hands. "I see what you're thinking, and you need to cut that shit out right now. Just because there was a reason I came back doesn't mean each word I've said hasn't been the God's honest truth. When I was given my orders, I thought I could keep my feelings in check, but that was a joke. That same night I was told to protect you, I watched you in your studio painting and knew I'd never be strong enough to stay away from you again. One look was all it took."

"You were in my house watching me paint?" I balked,

pulling back from his hold, trying to remember when it could have happened.

His face contorted in confusion. "I don't think that's all that relevant, considering everything else we're talking about here."

I shook my head, trying to focus my thoughts after he'd caught me off guard. "No, I know. You just surprised me. So our run-in at lunch and you showing up at dinner—those were attempts by my parents to bring us back together so you could protect me? You say you saw me and wanted more, but what does that even mean? What is it you want from me, Nico? A lot has changed since you left."

His eyes hardened just before he tugged me closer and slammed his lips down on mine. All thoughts and logic evaporated in a cloud of sultry smoke. No matter how much my mind tried to argue the dangers, my body was too desperate for his touch to care. It didn't matter that I had no experience to draw from, kissing Nico felt so natural, so right, that my body knew just how to move.

His hands grasped my ass and lifted me against him, pulling my dress up so I could wrap my legs around his narrow hips. Only once I was secure in his arms did he slowly pull away from our kiss. "I want everything from you, Sofia Genovese. I want your body and your mind. I want your secrets and your trust. I want to tell you every horrible thing I've ever done and know you'll love me anyway. I know it's going to take time for us to get there, and I'll have to work my ass off to earn it, but you're worth it. You were worth all the pain of walking away, and you're worth the groveling it may take to get you back. I didn't come near you all those years because I knew I'd never have the strength to stay away. I never once stopped thinking about you and never will. You're it for me, Ladybug. Let me show you how much I love you." He sucked my bottom lip between his, then nibbled on the soft flesh.

"Wait," I breathed, pulling my lips from his. "My parents are downstairs."

"Their bedroom is on the opposite end of the house."

"But it's still their house."

His eyes softened to a warm velvet. "It's the way it should have been—us as teenagers, sneaking away to explore one another. I think it's only right that it happens here." He didn't give me a chance to respond, but I couldn't have formed words if I'd wanted to. I was totally swept away with emotion.

Everything he'd said—it had filled the hole in my heart that never seemed to heal.

For a moment, I let myself believe that maybe, just maybe, there was a chance for us. That maybe the obstacles that sat in our way were surmountable. That maybe, I'd have my Nico back.

The temptation was too great.

I gave in to the sensations, rolling my hips to rub my core against his thick shaft straining against his pants.

He groaned, resting his forehead against mine. "I want to do this right. I've been fantasizing about it all night." Lowering me to my feet, Nico stepped back, eyeing me with a predator's gaze. Slowly, he stalked around behind me, stepping closer until I could feel his breath ghost across the skin on the back of my neck as his hands lower the zipper on my dress.

My body became overly sensitized; each hair stood on end, desperate for his touch. I couldn't believe this was happening, after so many years. It complicated matters, but I couldn't seem to care. I wanted Nico so badly my body ached for him.

"This is how it always should have been," he mused as his rough fingertips eased the straps of my dress off my shoulders. "You and me. We should have been each other's firsts— each other's one and only."

My belly dipped and swirled at his words, and his possible reaction to what I needed to tell him. "Um, actually, I'm not sure how to say this ... but I haven't ... been with anyone else. I've never done this," I whispered the words. I wasn't ashamed or embarrassed, but it felt awkward to say. I was a twenty-two-year-old virgin.

Nico went inhumanly still behind me. Suddenly self-conscious, I started to peek at him when his voice cracked out like a whip, startling me.

"On the bed."

I followed his order, crawling onto the full-size bed and turning to sit facing him, dressed only in the jeweled necklace. Nico unbuttoned his dress shirt, slipping the fabric from his muscular shoulders and revealing an assortment of tattoos as his steely gaze branded my flesh. The only light in the room was the soft glow from filtering in from outside, but it was plenty to confirm that his body was just as beautiful as I knew it would be. I wondered about his tattoos, wanting to hear the story behind each and trace the lines across his taut skin. The light was too dim to make out the details but enough to see how perfectly they complemented the contours of his sculpted body.

When he lowered his pants and boxer briefs, my mouth went dry. It was an odd sensation to see him stand before me, someone I had known so well, but who was so incredibly changed. He was all man now—no signs of the boy I'd known. Could he see the same was true for me—that the little girl he'd known was gone? Neither of us had survived our separation unscathed. Would our reunion be our undoing? Or would it make us stronger than we'd ever been before?

There was only one way to find out.

Nico lowered himself onto the bed, stalking up to where I lounged back on my elbows. "This body is mine," he rumbled as he eased himself over me. "These breasts," he murmured before grazing his teeth against my skin. "These ribs ..." His tongue explored the dips and valleys of my rib cage. "This belly ..." Soft kisses trailed one lower than the next. "And this pussy ... they're mine." He spread me apart and took a long, languorous lick up my slit, sending sparks of electric sensation throughout my body.

"Nico!" I gasped, arching with the need to be touched.

"That's it, baby. I want to hear you say my name. I want you to know who owns this body because no one else will ever fucking touch it." He dived in, circling my clit with his tongue while his fingers pulled at my hardened nipple. Each sensation alone would have been blissful, but together, they were mind-bending. He licked and sucked, growling when I moaned and twisting my nipples extra hard when I squirmed too much. He played my body like the keys of his piano, a masterful musician, my moans and gasps his symphony.

When I came, it was nothing like I'd been able to give myself with my own fingers. Never had I been remotely tempted to make noise when I touched myself, but the orgasm Nico drew from me had me biting off a strangled cry. Somewhere in the back of my mind, I knew I was at my parents' house and needed to be quiet, but it was nearly impossible.

The thundering waves of pleasure tore through my body like a tsunami, annihilating everything in its path. Every inch of my body was swimming in sensation; even my ears buzzed from the electric surge.

He drew every last ounce of pleasure from me, only stopping when I floated back down to earth. As I recovered, he eased himself over me, bringing us face to face, skin to skin.

"You are the most beautiful thing I've ever seen in my life. I should keep you locked in my bedroom, naked and writhing just like this, every day, all day." The heat in his eyes and need in his voice stirred to life a spark of sensation in my belly that I thought had surely burned itself out.

"You're not so bad to look at yourself. Will you tell me about these one day?" I asked, tracing the lines of his shoulder tattoo.

"I'll tell you anything you want, but first, I need to be inside you. I've never gone without a condom, so I'm clean. I want to be bare inside you with nothing between us." He peered at me in question, allowing me to make the call.

"What about pregnancy?" I asked cautiously, noting he hadn't raised that concern.

"I can't imagine anything finer than having you round with my child, so that's not a concern of mine."

Holy shit. He was serious.

"I'm on birth control," I whispered.

His eyes softened. "Another time then. For now, this is just about us. You're perfectly slick and ready, but it'll probably still hurt a bit. I can't say I'm sorry. Knowing I'm about to take your innocence makes me happier than you can fathom." His lips lowered to mine, kissing me passionately while one of his hands guided my knees up and back, opening me to him. His tip pressed inside me, warm and thick, spreading my entrance until I stiffened with worry. "Relax, Ladybug. It'll hurt more if you're tense. Try to remember it's me and how you were made for me."

I nodded, trying to ease my clenched muscles. Nico continued to rock himself just inside my entrance, allowing me to adjust to the sensation. Then, without warning, he thrust fully inside me, sending a stab of shooting pain through my core. I cried out, and he pulled my face close to his.

"Shhhh, that's it. It's over now. The pain is done," he soothed me, trailing his fingers up and down my arm.

As I calmed from the surprise, I noted that Nico's voice sounded strained. "Are you okay?" I asked warily. I didn't think I was doing anything wrong, but what did I know?

He chuckled, then kissed me lazily. "I'm more than okay. You're so fuckin' tight that I could die right now as the happiest man alive."

I smiled shyly just as Nico started to slowly rock inside me. I expected it to hurt, and there was a dull soreness, but it quickly eased into something more pleasurable.

"I'm not going to last, Sof. I've waited so long for this moment, and I can't hold back." His voice shook with strain, and I soared at knowing I affected him so deeply.

Only a couple of minutes after entering me, Nico's body broke out in a sheen of sweat and flexed tightly as he sucked in a breath and moaned his release. He took several ragged breaths as he recovered, then buried his face in my neck. "I promise it'll be better next time," he muttered against the skin of my neck.

I giggled, enjoying the feel of his weight over me. "What makes you think there was anything wrong with that?"

He lifted his head and gazed warmly at me in the dark room. "Trust me, it gets a whole lot better. I'm going to teach you, and I look forward to every one of our lessons." He grinned deviously, then pulled my back flush against his chest, which was a huge relief. His words had triggered a flood of emotion as I began to grasp the implications of what we'd done. He thought this was a beginning—not just a one-time thing. I had known he would, and a part of me wanted that too, but it wasn't so simple.

A relationship with Nico would be complicated.

I wasn't even sure it was possible.

Yes, we had a connection, which included amazing chemistry, but that didn't change the past. His departure set into motion a chain of events that couldn't be undone, nor did I want it to.

As I listened to Nico's breathing slip into the restful pattern of sleep, I lay awake worrying about what I'd done. Even if I could wash away the hurt from years ago, being with Nico would be enormously complicated. He was under the impression we'd patched things between us and all was well, but the reality was my troubles had only just begun.

CHAPTER 16
Sofia

THEN

Thursday and Friday after Nico's birthday, he didn't show up at school. I texted and called him repeatedly with no response. On Saturday morning, I had my mom drive me to his house only to find no one home. Just after lunch, I finally got a text from him.

Come to Josh Newton's party tonight, we can talk there.

A party? We'd never gone to any of the high school parties. At least I hadn't gone. It was possible he went without me, but I highly doubted it.

I was anxious to see Nico, but equally hesitant. That sixth sense that resides deep inside us, the one that stirs to life when a loved one is in trouble or a natural disaster occurs, was telling me something wasn't right. It made me want to hide under the covers of my bed and not come out, but that wasn't an option. I needed to know what the hell was going on.

After some negotiating, I was able to convince Maria to sneak me out of the house and drop me off at the party. Her reticence to help me had nothing to do with disobeying my parents and everything to do with carving time out of her busy schedule to bother with me. I didn't care, as long as I found a way to get to Nico.

It was a good thing the houses weren't close together in Josh's neighborhood because the music from inside his house could be heard all the way down the street. Maria dropped me at the curb and drove off without looking back. I hurried to the house and let myself inside into a chaotic swarm of bodies. The house was big enough that kids weren't packed together, but they were everywhere—dancing, talking, making out. Near the entry, a table was set up for beer pong with a dozen or so people crowded around it. I cautiously walked past, searching the crowd for the only face I was interested in seeing.

A couple of girls I was casual friends with ran over to greet me, surprised I had come to the party. They confirmed they had seen Nico, so he was there somewhere. Continuing my search, I wound my way toward the back of the house. Unlike our parties at home, the doors to family rooms were not closed, and I was subjected to public displays I had no desire to see.

My stomach slowly rose into my throat. If Nico was at the party but not with the main partygoers out front, did that mean he was back here in a private room? It wasn't possible. He would never do that to me. Yet that sixth sense pulsed louder and louder in my ears until it drowned out the music and the pounding of my heart was all I could hear. I should turn back and run. Nothing good could come from finishing my search, but I was compelled forward. I stepped mechanically into the doorway of the last door on the left and took in the scene before me, my heart splintering into shards at my feet.

Nico stood facing me, his head thrown back in pleasure as one hand steadied himself against the wall and the other held the head of a blonde on her knees, her head bobbing before him. My body betrayed me, freezing me to the spot, forcing me to witness his blatant infidelity to the bond between us.

As if sensing the destruction he was causing, Nico's eyes slowly opened as his head came forward. None of the surprise or remorse I had expected were present, adding another blow to the gaping hole in my chest. He knew exactly what he was doing, and he didn't care.

Confusion over encountering this alternate reality made my head swim with dizziness.

This couldn't be real. There had to be some supernatural explanation.

But there wasn't.

It was real—just like when Marco was killed.

Every second was real and seared into my brain.

"*Why?*" I gasped as I braced myself against the doorframe.

Nico tugged at the girl's hair, pulling her lips off him, and tucked himself casually back in his pants. When the girl turned to see what was going on, I realized it was Brooke Britton, one of the cattiest, most heartless of the Xavier cheerleaders. She smiled snidely at me, winked at Nico, and left the room, bumping my shoulder on her way out.

"We aren't kids anymore, Sofia," Nico said coldly. "You can't just follow me around like a lost puppy and expect me to hang onto you forever, passing notes and holding hands. This isn't working for me anymore."

Not working for him? Where was this coming from? Was this because I stopped him from going further on our date? How could he be breaking things off between us when he was just professing his feelings for me days before? And why did he have a black eye and a split lip? None of it made any sense—my traumatized brain could hardly process the information.

"Why are you doing this? What … what happened to you?" I stuttered out, my words a jumbled mess in my head.

"Life happened. We all grow up sometime, and that some-time is now. I've decided to go into boxing. I'm good at it and can make a shit ton of money. You know I don't want to end up in debt like my dad, and boxing will get me there. I'm quit-ting school, and this little thing between us is over. My life is headed in a new direction, and it doesn't include you." His eyes were cut shards of glass as he spoke, each word more resolute than the last.

He reached out to grab his jacket off a nearby chair with a slight wobble. Was he drunk? I'd never known Nico to drink, and now I was wondering if I ever knew Nico at all. Was this a show put on for me, or had he always worn a mask to hide the monster underneath? We all had secrets. We all wore masks. Which Nico was the real one and which was the front?

"Stop this!" I finally shot back at him, charging over to where he stood. "I don't know what's gotten into you, but you need to stop *right fucking now*. It's not you, and I know it." I punctuated my words by slamming my hands against his broad chest over and over.

Nico grabbed my wrists, stopping me mid-tantrum. "This *is* the real me. If you can't accept that, you're in for a world of pain. Brooke's not the first, and she won't be the last, so I suggest you get over your little crush and move on." He flung my hands out to the sides and charged past me, leaving me drowning in his wake.

The deep waters of grief and devastation surged up around me, causing my knees to buckle. I dropped to the floor, my lungs convulsing with painful sobs—like I was breathing underwater, choking and coughing but finding no relief.

Nico Conti didn't just break my heart; he destroyed it.

If anyone came in search of a vacant room and spotted me weeping on the floor, they didn't make themselves known, and I didn't care if anyone witnessed my undoing.

I didn't care about anything anymore.

Once a soothing numbness settled inside me, I picked myself up, found a back exit from the house, and left. The early April night was chilly, but I didn't notice. I walked home in the dark, unaware of any lurking dangers. Or maybe I was aware, and in my broken mental state, I was inviting them to put me out of my misery. Regardless, it was not to be that night. I made it home safely, shaking from head to toe.

After letting myself in the side door, I disarmed the alarm, then walked in a haze upstairs. I don't know why I did it—it wasn't something I did consciously—but I opened the door to Marco's room and crawled into his empty bed. Maybe it was my imagination, but I swore I could still smell him on the pillow. Wrapped in the imaginary arms of my big brother, I drifted into a dreamless sleep.

WHAT DID you say to someone who'd thrown you away? Did you beg them to come back? Or did you recognize that it wasn't meant to be and move on? I wasn't the type of girl to beg, but my relationship with Nico went too far back to give up without a fight.

True to his word, he never came back to school. For weeks I tried to talk to him—texting, phone calls, and even dropping by his parents' house—all without any luck.

He was a ghost, as if he'd never even existed.

His departure didn't just leave me with heartache; it also sparked the wrath of Brooke Britton. She waged a war against me, blaming me for Nico leaving school. I was pretty sure it was just an excuse, but that didn't matter. She took every opportunity she could to make my life a living hell.

On top of dealing with my grief and hurt, I was bullied on a daily basis. While in PE, my school clothes would end up mysteriously soaked in my locker. If I wasn't careful, I'd get an elbow to the ribs walking down the hall or a tray of food dropped over my head in the cafeteria. Each day was a new torment, making me more miserable than I already was.

I began to dread lunch and classroom transitions. Nico had been such a large part of my world that I'd had no need for other friends. There were girls I had talked to in classes, but no one I was close with. When he left, I was all alone. In a school full of wealthy, privileged kids, I became an easy target. I tried to stand up for myself at first, but it only made things worse—as if Brooke fed on the conflict.

One day, I was walking with my lunch to the far table where I sat each day alone, and a foot shot out, sending me flailing to the ground on top of my tray of food. Roars of laughter filled the room. I slowly stood, relieved that my sister didn't have the same lunch period and couldn't see my utter humiliation. I didn't look for the culprit or make eye contact with anyone as I stood, pulling my slice of pizza off my chest.

Just as I started to walk away, a guy I wasn't familiar with walked over and motioned for me to stay still. His black hair fell into his eyes, and his uniform tie was pulled loose with his collar unbuttoned—a violation of the dress code. Whoever he was, he wasn't interested in fitting in.

He reached over and yanked a kid up out of his seat at the end of the table, fist wrapped in the kid's collar. "You fucking touch her again … any of you," he said, slowly glancing at the others at the table, "and I will make you wish you'd never been born. Understood?" His voice was an angry warning without a hint of doubt or restraint.

"You can't just threaten us," spat Brooke, seated at the table with the boy who'd tripped me.

The guy let go of his target, slowly turning to Brooke. "Are you going to stop me, Brooke?" he asked in an eerily quiet voice. "Maybe ask your daddy, the politician, to go after me? Or maybe James here, whose dad sits in front of a news camera every night at six. Maybe he'll have his daddy report me on the news? The thing is, Brooke, I don't give a shit about that stuff. I don't care who your parents are or what they do for a living, but I do know that I've always come out of a fight on top. So, if you want to take it outside and settle things the traditional way, I'm more than happy. Otherwise, leave. Her. The. Fuck. Alone." Not waiting for a response, he ushered me toward the table where I normally sat before dropping his backpack on the bench. "Stay here. I'll be right back."

I had no idea what was going on, but I was more than happy to accept his help. I sat at the table trying to ignore all the stares and prying eyes while I waited for the stranger to come back. When he did, he put a single tray down between us piled with pizza and two apples. Normally, we were only allowed one slice at a time, but clearly, the rules didn't apply to him.

"Eat," he said before taking a large bite of pizza.

I picked up a slice but paused before taking a bite. "I'm a little embarrassed. You stuck your neck out for me, and I don't even know your name."

"Michael," he said while chewing, then smirked as his eyes lit with amusement. "Guy looked like he was gonna piss himself."

I couldn't help the relieved laughter that bubbled up from deep inside me. "You're pretty intimidating. I'm surprised I haven't noticed you around here. You don't exactly blend in."

"I just started at the semester break. You may not have noticed me, but I've seen how they've been treating you lately. You piss in someone's cornflakes?"

"It might be easier to take if I *had* done something—at least then I'd know it was my own fault—but no. Brooke started it, and I seem to have become everyone's favorite pastime."

"It started when the guy you were always with moved away, right?" He asked the question casually, unaware of the stab of pain his words caused.

My gaze dropped to the table, and I lowered the pizza, suddenly uninterested in eating. "Yeah, that was Nico."

Michael's chewing slowed, his eyes narrowing. "Something happen to him?"

"Not exactly. He left, and we didn't part on good terms. It's been hard on me."

"Well, I can't help with that, but I can keep those dickheads off your back."

I offered him a small smile, suddenly exhausted from the ebbing adrenaline. We finished our lunch together, getting to know one another, and slipped into an easy friendship.

Each day, he joined me for lunch and talked to me in the halls. Like me, he didn't seem to have other friends. It wasn't at all the same as what I shared with Nico, but it helped to dull the pain. I was sure Michael sensed I was a little broken, but he never brought it up. He was the buoy in the middle of my storm, and I clung to him for dear life.

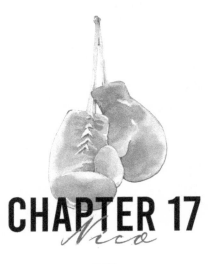

CHAPTER 17
Nico

NOW

The thrill of reuniting with Sofia was doused in a bucket of ice water when I woke alone the next morning. I quickly dressed and went in search for her but found her mother instead. Carlotta hid her surprise at seeing me, informing me that Sofia had stepped out. I excused myself with what little pride I had left and slunk from the house.

Talk about awkward.

At least it hadn't been Enzo. I had known I was taking a chance by staying the night with his daughter right under his roof, but there was no way I was letting her slip away from me. When I told her what had happened, her protective barrier visibly crumbled. I had unguarded access to my Sofia, the girl who had loved me unconditionally, and I wasn't wasting the opportunity.

Being with Sofia was as perfect as I'd always imagined. I

only wished she'd stayed with me the entire night. Clearly, we still had some work to do.

What the fuck happened? Why did she run from me?

After returning home to shower and change, I sat in my car outside the meet location and racked my brain about what had gone wrong. Had she been upset, and I was too lust-crazed to notice? How could she welcome me inside her when she'd never been with anyone else, then leave without a word? The way I'd broken things off with her had been horrific, but if that was the issue, why did she have sex with me at all?

None of it made any sense, and it was pissing me off. I wanted more than anything to find her and demand answers, but we had our meeting with the Russians, and I couldn't miss it. Despite my oath, Sofia would always come first. However, I wouldn't break my promise to the family unless it was necessary. There would be plenty of time for answers.

The other thing that had gnawed at me all morning was Sofia's safety. If I didn't know where she'd run off to, I couldn't keep her safe. When I finally got my hands on her, we'd have more than one topic to discuss. I was pleased to have been included in our meeting with the Russians, but considering everything else I had going on, I was also anxious to get it over with so I could sort out the rest of my shit.

I'd received a text an hour before from Enzo telling me the location and time for the meet. The address took me to a run-down part of Brooklyn where the old brick buildings had seen their day. Wealthy investors hadn't yet seized the properties to revitalize the area, so the neighborhood remained much as it had been for decades.

I didn't have to wait long before Gabe's car pulled up followed by a second vehicle. He and Enzo stepped from his black Lincoln Town Car along with two soldiers, and four more exited from the other car. I joined them, shaking hands with Gabe and Enzo and nodding to the others—all of us equally stoic. Meets were supposed to be violence-free, but there were never any guarantees.

As we greeted one another, a large metal garage door slid open. A single soldier stood at the entry, inviting us inside. The building housed a typical mechanic's garage that I would have bet was a chop shop. The little garage tucked away in Brooklyn would be the perfect place to take stolen cars and refurbish them to be sold on the black market.

We were led to the back of the building and down a hallway past a series of offices to a small conference room. Three men were seated at an oval table along with half a dozen soldiers at their backs. As we filed into the room, the three men slowly stood, and we all eyed each other warily.

"Gabe," greeted the man in the middle in a heavy Russian accent. "And this must be the elusive Enzo Genovese. We appreciate you joining us today." It wasn't surprising the man was able to pick out Enzo. He was the oldest among us, implying higher rank, but he also had a commanding air that left no question about his powerful station.

"I appreciate you giving us the opportunity to discuss business and hopefully work through this little mess."

"Yes, of course. These things happen. Please, have a seat."

With our soldiers standing at our backs, we joined the Russians at the glass-topped conference table. The room was saturated with the stale odor of foreign cigarettes—no Marlboro Lights for the bratva. Between the vodka and tobacco, it was a miracle any of them lived past fifty. Their faces were weathered and harsh, hands dotted with old tattoos, and their teeth were stained a putrid yellow. These men were old-school bratva—the equivalent of our Italian Zips who came over from Sicily. They had yet to enter the modern age, still living under the archaic rules of the past.

The leader, Boris "Biba" Mikhailov, leaned back confidently in his chair. "I understand you have a traitor on your hands."

"Yes," conceded Enzo. "My underboss Sal has betrayed me and injured my reputation with a number of my associates, such as yourself. He's on the run, but we'll find him."

Biba tsked, shaking his head. "Is not good for business to have such a trusted comrade turn on you. It does not instill ... confidence in your operation."

The blatant disrespect made me wish I could hop over the table and teach Biba some manners. Ever the businessman, Enzo didn't even look fazed by the Russian's slight.

"That is a matter I'm working to correct. I understand Sal entered an arrangement with you on behalf of the Lucciano family. I'm here to see what we can do to keep our end of that bargain."

"Da, da. We have a shipment of guns that has yet to be paid for. Five hundred K." He lifted a brow in challenge.

"It was my understanding the amount owed was two fifty."

"There have been ... complications in holding the shipment past the scheduled delivery date. The price has gone up." His eyes sparked with amusement, and several of his soldiers behind him smirked. Every man in that room knew his excuse was bullshit—there were no complications. The Russians just wanted to milk us for every dollar they could get.

Enzo's jaw flexed almost imperceptibly. "Alright, but I

need to find a buyer. If you can give me until the end of the week, we have a deal."

Biba gave a contemplative frown, glancing at his cohort beside him. "Da, this will work."

Simultaneously, both groups rose from the table. Enzo reached out, extending his hand to Biba. "It's good doing business with you, Boris."

"Always a pleasure, my friend." He pulled away, still holding Enzo's gaze. "I hope you are aware, Sal's betrayal was a slight to us as well. I have men searching for him—if we find him before you, he is ours to make a lesson of. It cannot be known that someone has screwed the bratva and walked away." Biba's eyes were suddenly crystal clear, a deadly promise in his harsh stare.

"I would expect nothing less. All I ask is, should you find him first, you let me know so I can call off my own search."

The Russian's lips pulled back in a wide grin for the first time. "Of course, then we agree. Before you go, we must toast." One of the soldiers magically appeared with a full bottle of vodka and a stack of shot glasses. Crazy fucking Russians—not even fazed by the fact that it was ten in the morning.

Biba poured healthy portions of the clear liquid into each glass. "You'll like this. It's Beluga, some of the finest from Mother Russia." He kept the bottle in one hand, then lifted his glass in the other, and we all followed suit. "To continued friendships and common goals," he said with a crazy gleam in his eye. Sal was dead no matter who found him, but if it was the Russians, he was going to wish for death long before it came.

All of us threw back our shots, knowing it was rude in

Russian culture not to down your offering in one swallow. Biba handed the bottle to his soldier, then led us out of the conference room. As I walked in line back down the hallway, I glanced inside one of the open offices and stuttered to a stop. On the floor, leaned against a row of metal filing cabinets, was a painting of three skulls.

It was identical to the piece I watched Sofia painting.

What were the chances? Zero.

A hand shot out, grabbing the doorknob and pulling the door closed. One of Biba's soldiers narrowed his eyes at me. "I believe you were leaving," he snapped in warning.

"My apologies," I offered, turning to catch up with the others.

I only half listened as we said our farewells, then went our separate ways. I started my car and began to drive with no destination in mind.

It couldn't be. It had to be a coincidence.

The image of Sofia's panicked face when I told her I'd watched her paint came to mind, and my temples began to throb. Why on earth would Sofia's painting be at a Russian chop shop? What the fuck had I missed in her life while I'd been gone?

She had known about her family mafia connections all her life, so what other secrets did she have? The fucking Russians? Those assholes were insane. What could she possibly be thinking by associating with them?

My mind was utterly blown.

I needed to figure out what the hell was going on, and I need to know *now*.

CHAPTER 18
Sofia

THEN

"I'm so ready to get out of my parents' house. Two whole years until I graduate … I'm never going to make it," I told Michael in a huff. We had come outside for our lunch on an unusually warm spring day, making ourselves comfortable in a patch of sun on campus grounds.

"Yeah, well, my dad found me this weekend," he said, pulling a blade of grass and slowly tearing it into pieces.

"He found you? What do you mean he found you? Were you hidden?"

He peered up at me through his thick lashes and smirked. "Sort of. We told everyone my parents had just divorced when I moved out here, but that wasn't the case. My parents were never married. My dad is a dangerous man. He's part of the Russian mob, the bratva."

Despite the warmth of the sun, goose bumps rose along

the length of my arms. "Are you joking with me?" My mood had gone so severe, Michael perked up at attention.

His eyes narrowed as he searched my face. "I'm not joking, Sof. I shouldn't even have told you, but it's not like I have anyone else to talk to about it."

"You were on the run from him?"

"Not exactly. If that was the case, we probably would have moved a hell of a lot farther away. A few years ago, my dad made it known he wanted me to follow in his footsteps, and my mom freaked. She made a plan, got us fake papers, and moved us out here. All of her family is in New York, so she didn't want to go far, but she hoped to keep my dad away from me."

"Papers—like a new identity? Is your name even Michael?" I gaped, having trouble comprehending what he was telling me. What were the chances the guy who had become my closest friend over the past year was connected to the Russian mob? The Italian and Russian factions didn't exactly mix, as far as I could tell. I had yet to run into any Russian speakers in my neighborhood of Staten Island.

Michael grinned deviously. "Technically, it's Mikhail Savin —my mom calls me Misha. Garin is a short form of my grandfather's name, Gerasim."

As if telling me his favorite food or his plans for the week-end, Michael had volunteered a deeply personal secret. I was floored. Never in all my years had anyone opened up to me with something so important, trusting me with such sensitive information.

"My dad is an Italia Mafia boss," I blurted without any hesitation. My eyes grew wide as I realized what I'd done. There was no taking the words back. All those years of keeping the secret to myself, and I let the bomb drop without a second thought. I was completely dumbfounded.

Michael stared at me, then threw back his head in a fit of laughter.

"You're laughing? I'm not joking!" I hissed at him, slapping his leg.

"I know, that's why it's so funny. I could tell you were different than the other paper doll cutouts here, but I had no idea we were such kindred spirits."

I couldn't help but grin at his amusement and shake my head. "So glad I have a partner in the Fucked-Up Family Club —or should I say comrade?"

"Oh! Sofia's got jokes!" he teased, still smiling broadly. "You can use whatever word you want, but I don't speak Russian."

"Guess that makes sense—I don't speak Italian. I take it your mom is Russian?"

"Yeah, but she was born here. So was my dad."

"Tell me about him," I said, growing more somber. "What does it mean that he's found you?"

Michael shrugged, attempting to look nonchalant, but I could sense his unease. "He was pissed at my mom, but he's not a terrible guy. He's not going to hurt her or anything. He's insisting I spend some weekends with him in the city, so I'm not sure exactly what it means. He was never super involved in my life, and I certainly never had contact with his bratva dealings. Your guess is as good as mine."

"But you're going to still live here, though, right?" The thought of him leaving terrified me. Not because he'd kept the bullies at bay, but because he was the only person who saw me —saw the real me.

"I'm not going anywhere, Sof. No worries." He gazed at me, almost sadly. "Mafia, huh. One obstacle after another," he muttered to himself.

"What do you mean?"

"Nothing, just talking to myself." He smiled, but I could still see that sadness lurking in his eyes. "Your Nico, did he know about your family?" he asked quietly. It was one of only a handful of times he'd ever brought up Nico in the year we'd been friends, and the mention caught me off guard.

"Ah ... no. No one knows. In fact, my family doesn't know that I know." My gaze dropped to the ground where I studied the dirt on my shoe.

He was silent, so I dared a peek up. Michael's eyes were bulging round. "You serious? They didn't *tell* you? How on earth did you figure it out?"

"It's a long story, but my brother was killed when I was young. My parents lied about what had happened. After that, I watched and learned. It wasn't all that hard when you actually pay attention."

A sly smile spread across his face. "Atta girl. No pulling the wool over Sofia's eyes."

I chuckled, appreciating his ability to lighten the mood. That was how it always was with Michael—effortless. Our friendship came naturally, and even heavy subjects never felt all that burdensome. I wished I could allow him to slip into that hole Nico had left in my heart, but it had been barricaded shut.

I couldn't do it.

I feared only one man would ever fit into the misshaped organ in my chest, and that man was gone. Fortunately, Michael never took our friendship that route. I wasn't sure if he sensed my reluctance or if it was for other reasons, but I certainly wasn't going to bring up the subject and ask. I was just glad I had him in my life and didn't want to do anything to disrupt that.

FOR TWO MORE YEARS, Michael and I maintained our easy friendship. Just to be safe, we kept our relationship under wraps. He didn't come to my parents' house and didn't mention me on trips into the city with his father. The dynamic worked for us, and it wasn't until the end of our senior year that things unexpectedly changed.

I was lined up to start at Columbia in the fall, and Michael was debating whether to go to work for his father. His mom hated the idea, but she couldn't do anything about it. The prospect of the bratva hadn't bothered me all that much. Watching my family all those years, I knew he could live an essentially normal life whether he was in the bratva or out. I was just glad he talked to me about it and included me in his life, even the darker parts.

As seniors, we were exempt from our last round of finals, so the administration had planned to take us on one last field trip into the city to visit the Met, otherwise known as the Metropolitan Museum of Art. I'd been countless times in my life, but I always enjoyed going. Between the sheer size of the place and the traveling exhibits, there was always something new to see.

The buses were scheduled to leave first thing that Friday morning, but Michael was late to our homeroom class. I texted him, pissed he was going to miss the trip, but never got a response. It wasn't until we were lining up to get on the bus that he came running over.

"Where the hell have you been?" I fussed at him, punching him in his chest.

Michael winced and stepped back, his shoulders curving in protectively. "Fuck, Sof, that hurt."

"What are you talking about? I barely touched you. What's going on?" I might as well have just slapped a bug away, so there was no way it should have hurt.

He recovered quickly, smirking. "I'll tell you once we're on the bus." He motioned for me to hurry on board and then followed me.

I found a seat in the back and waited until the bus began to move before insisting on some answers. "Spill."

"Demanding today, aren't we?" Grinning, he turned his body to cage me in against the window, then unbuttoned his uniform dress shirt. Beneath, a gauzy white bandage was adhered to his chest. He slowly peeled back the tape, revealing an intricate tattoo of an angel inked over his entire left pectoral. The angel's wings curved around her protectively as she sat naked on the ground, her face shielded by her arms.

"It's absolutely stunning," I breathed, in awe of the delicate artistry used to create such a beautiful rendering on human skin. Then I remember how I'd punched him. "Oh my God," I gasped, hands flying to my mouth. "I'm so sorry I hit you! I had no idea."

"It's fine, Sof. Look, it's not even bleeding or anything."

I studied the tattoo, taking in each fine line and the intricate detail. "Did you just get it last night?"

He nodded sheepishly. "It's symbolic of being a part of the bratva—a commitment to thievery."

"Is it official? You joined?" I gaped at him, stunned he would take that step without saying something to me first.

"Not quite," he said, resetting the patch over his healing skin. "No matter if I officially join their ranks, the bratva will always be a part of my life because of my father."

I nodded in perfect understanding. When something like that touched your life, there was no escaping it. Whether in small ways like fearing the police, or in a more concrete fashion like hoarding money and carrying weapons. The mentality of a criminal bled into your subconscious, changing the way you thought.

"Did you show your mom?" She hated that he was involved with the bratva in any way.

His lips thinned, eyes hardening. "No. I know what her response will be, and I don't feel like fighting with her. That's just about all we do anymore. I hate it. I know she wants the best for me, but I just don't see myself in an office job working an eight-to-five for the rest of my life. That's just not me."

"You could play piano or do something else legitimate that isn't a standard job. That way you and your mom could both be happy."

"I could," he conceded, eyes drifting out the window. "There's still time to decide what I'm doing long-term. Despite my mom's beliefs otherwise, my dad isn't forcing me into anything."

"I wish I could say the same. I'm not sure what four years at college is going to do for me when all I want to do is paint for a living, but Dad doesn't see it that way. He's adamant that I attend college. At least he's letting me study art rather than forcing me to get some boring business degree."

"Hey, it's four more years that you get to dick around before you have to be an adult. I think that sounds like a sweet gig."

I raised a brow at him. "The same could be said for you. Why don't you go to school with me? Your grades are plenty good to get in."

"And pay them ungodly amounts of money just to sit in a classroom?" He gaped at me. "Hell, no."

"But there's no problem with me doing that?"

"Not when your dad wants to give them the money. It's not like he doesn't have the spare cash."

"Is that why you haven't planned to go to college? Is it the money?" His mom didn't have much money, but surely, his dad would help him go if it was important to him.

"Nah, it's just not me. I don't want to go, so there's no reason to throw the money away. But if you hit up any good college parties, you be sure to give me a call." He waggled his brows, making me snort with laughter.

We talked about our plans for the final weeks of school until the bus pulled up to the enormous stone museum. As seniors, we were given the leeway to wander the building on our own under strict instruction to return at the designated time. I dragged Michael off toward the modern and contemporary art wing—my favorite portion of the museum. The current exhibit was ultra-contemporary abstract art.

Not what I'd been hoping for.

Taking a detour, I led Michael to the adjacent collection of 19th and early 20th century European art, paying special attention to the post-impressionism pieces. They had a beautiful work by van Gogh called *Cypresses* that I took in for several long minutes.

"I've seen your work. You paint just as well as any of these people," muttered Michael with his eyes glued to his phone. Not as in tune to the art world, he had been busier playing a game on his phone than enjoying the exhibits.

"That's the plan. I want to sell my art for a living someday, but it's not an easy field to get into. Most of these artists died in poverty, their work only appreciated after their death," I mused, still lost in the swirling brushstrokes of van Gogh's piece.

"If they're so famous and too dead to enjoy it, you should just put their name on your work. It's not like schmucks on the street would know the difference." His head was down, oblivious of the impact his words had made until he glanced up and saw my wide eyes. "It was a joke, Sofia."

"My parents will be in the city tomorrow. I need you to come over so I can show you something."

Michael's eyes narrowed a fraction, and the corners of his lips twitched up. "What have you been hiding, naughty girl?"

"I'm not hiding anything! I just want to show you something. Don't be absurd." I grabbed his sleeve and tugged him on to the next exhibit, which was our general pattern for the rest of the day.

The following morning, I ushered Michael through the side door at my house, hoping no one would look at the security cameras stationed around our property. It was the first time he'd been to my house, and it was odd having him there.

"Great place. Very Mediterranean. Guess I shouldn't be surprised."

"Yeah, yeah. Follow me." I led him back to my studio, which was a mess of art supplies and canvases. As it was isolated at the far end of the house and a total disaster area, no one ventured back there but me. It was my sanctuary. I loved everything about the well-lit space.

I flipped through a pile of canvases leaned against the wall, pulling out the one I was looking for and placing it on an unoccupied easel. Michael and I both stared at the piece—the depiction of a European farming community situated beneath a mountain. Before he said a word, I handed him a rolled-up poster I pulled from beneath my supply table.

Unrolling it, he held the poster up, peering closely at the image, then back at my canvas. He searched and analyzed, comparing the two pieces. "This is remarkable," he said on a breath, never taking his eyes from his task. Finally, he lowered the poster and turned to me, his face as impassive as I'd ever seen it. "Sofia, I need to know why you showed me this."

I chewed on my lip, uncertain what I wanted to say. I hadn't been totally sure why I'd showed him what I'd done. Pride? To some extent. But it was also invigorating. There was a thrill in knowing I'd so masterfully copied a great work of art. "At the museum, you said I should put their names on my art. What if … I did? What if I made copies of famous artwork?"

"I think you'd be a very talented, very rich young woman, but is that what you really want?"

"One day, I was at a museum and had the same revelation you had yesterday. I can paint just as well as these other people. I came home with my poster and painted. Copying the detail, using aging techniques and specialized paints—it was the most exhilarating thing I'd ever done. I want to sell my own original pieces as well, but the thrill of creating this—I can't imagine topping it. I'd already been thinking about what piece I could do next."

"Are you saying, if I could find a buyer, you'd be interested in selling this work as an original Cézanne? There would be consequences if it were ever traced back to you. Surely, you understand that." He searched my features warily, trying to judge my willingness of conviction.

"The appealing part of it—the challenge—isn't in simply painting the piece. The satisfaction comes from successfully passing it off as the original. What's the point if it just sits in my closet? I want to know that I've created the ultimate forgery able to fool anyone who looks at it." My voice thrummed with excitement. "It's just like you said. This world becomes a part of us. The secrets and lies are in our blood. As much as I hate that my family has kept their secrets from me, I can't help but delight in having secrets of my own. Call me a hypocrite, I don't really care." I smiled at Michael, who happened to be one of those very secrets.

He took in the glint in my eye and smiled mischievously. "In that case, I think this could be the start of a beautiful arrangement. I'll talk to my father and see who he knows."

"My father would lose his shit if he found out I was working with Russians."

"Sof, you've kept your secrets your whole life. There's no reason he should ever have to know. My father's people won't have any idea who my source is. This will be our little secret." He winked, then tossed the poster back onto the table. "Now let's eat. I'm starved."

It was my turn to throw back my head and laugh, feeling more alive than I could ever recall feeling. The completed painting had been sitting in my studio for weeks. I hadn't had a concrete plan what to do with it. Like I'd told Michael, initially, I had painted it purely as a personal challenge. Once it was complete and I realized how perfectly I'd duplicated the original, I started to imagine the possibilities.

Dangerous, thrilling possibilities.

That was as far as I'd entertained the idea, unsure if I was willing or able to take it any further. When Michael made his comment at the museum, it felt like fate—like all the crazy events of my life were actually the carefully placed stepping-stones leading me to that specific place in time. My brother's death opening my eyes to my family's secrets and leading me to Nico. Nico's departure bringing Michael into my life. At the time, the two greatest sorrows of my life seemed insurmountable. But each had been instrumental in getting me to where I was—strong and confident.

A woman who knew what she wanted.

A woman with a taste for the darker side of life.

OVER THE NEXT FOUR YEARS, Michael acted as my broker in our lucrative partnership. Of course, it hadn't been about the money. My parents had set up trust funds for all of us girls. I appreciated knowing I'd made my own money, but the business was more than that.

It was my passion.

I loved creating unique art of my own, but there was nothing like the thrill of duplicating a world-renown master-piece. I adored my work and had no intention of quitting. Even if my family had no problem with my activities, they would be furious with my choice of partners. Fortunately, they thought I was the perfect little angel Sofia, and I was happy to support that misconception as long as possible.

Michael and I remained as close as ever, although we didn't see each other all that often while I was at school. We tried to have lunch on occasion, but we were both busy. He'd taken on a more active role with his father's business, acquiring the eight-pointed stars of the bratva when he'd taken his oath. One by one, he'd obtained dozens of tattoos that blended into an intricate human work of art.

He might have been enormously intimidating to anyone else, but to me, he was freedom and acceptance personified. I didn't care what faction he joined or how many tattoos he got, and he accepted me for every one of my flaws and idiosyncrasies. We were a team—a package deal—and I wasn't about to let anyone tear us apart.

CHAPTER 19
Sofia

NOW

I successfully avoided Nico for two whole days. He had texted and called—presumably acquiring my number from my parents—but I hadn't read the messages or listened to his voicemails. I knew I was acting childish, but I didn't know how to handle the situation, so I'd simply avoided it.

After having sex with Nico, I had laid in bed wide-awake with his arm draped over me for hours. When I couldn't take it any longer, I slipped from the bed and headed for the living room. I managed a few hours of sleep on the sofa, then fled to Starbucks the moment the sun began to rise. I'd done more thinking in two days' time than I had in my whole lifetime, and I still had no idea what to do.

I was relieved when my boss asked me to come into work on Monday morning. The gallery wasn't open, but there was always a mountain of paperwork to be done. My boss had a great eye for art and was loads of fun to be around, but he sucked at the administrative aspects of running a gallery. I spent an hour or so rifling through papers and listening to Miles chatter about his weekend when I heard a knock on the glass door. My heart nearly leaped out of my chest at the thought of Nico catching up with me, but I quickly relaxed when I saw Michael peeking through the tinted glass.

Unlocking the deadbolt, I ushered him inside. "Hey, Michael. What's up?"

"Is that Michael?" called Miles from around the corner. "If I'd known having you here would bring Michael around more often, I would have hired you sooner." Miles winked at me as he walked over, then gave Michael a hug. "What brings you in?"

"It's good to see you, Miles. I just needed to have a word with Sofia, if you aren't too busy."

"Not at all! We were getting some housekeeping stuff done —nothing super important. You two need me, I'll be back here buried in the storage closet. If I'm not back in half an hour, send help." He grabbed a clipboard and disappeared around the corner.

"Is everything okay?" I asked quietly.

"Yeah, don't worry. I wanted you to know I did some digging on that detective you talked to, and it looks like he wasn't a cop. My sources at the city had no record of a James Breechner—nor could I find anything at the state or fed level. Did he show you a badge or any form of identification?"

"No, I can't believe I didn't ask for that. Who the hell do you think he is?"

"No idea. If you see him again, call me immediately. I have eyes out for him, but you be extra cautious, okay?"

I nodded distractedly, still trying to imagine who Breechner worked for and why he'd sought me out.

"Hey, look at me," Michael called to me softly, drawing my eyes back to his. "I'm sure this has nothing to do with you. He was probably just questioning you because he saw us together."

"That's supposed to make me feel better?" I teased with a hint of sarcasm. "I don't want someone after you any more than I do me."

"It should make you feel better. I can take care of myself—promise. I figured you knew that by now." He gave me a smirk, but it didn't lighten my mood as intended.

"Doesn't mean I'm not going to worry about you."

"Don't take this the wrong way, but you're not exactly the type to sit at home and worry. You sure there isn't something else bothering you?"

I let out a deep breath, my shoulders sagging. "Nico showed up last week."

Michael's eyebrows nearly touched his hairline. "No shit! How'd that go?"

"Well …"

Muttering from the other room interrupted me just as I started to speak.

"Can we talk about it over breakfast tomorrow? It's complicated, and I'd rather not share with the world."

"Of course. How about Sarabeth's at eight?"

"Perfect. I appreciate you stopping by to let me know what you found."

"Absolutely. I'll see you in the morning." He tapped my nose with his knuckle and breezed out of the gallery.

I tried not to spend the rest of the day worrying about the

fake cop or Nico, but it was exhausting. By the time I ran a few errands and got back to my parents' house that evening, the only thing I wanted to do was paint. I tossed my keys on the bench, ran upstairs to change into sweats, and then headed for my sanctuary.

Flipping on the light in my studio, I screeched when I found Nico leaning against the far wall. "What the hell? Just because you work for my dad doesn't mean you can just let yourself in whenever."

"Is that what I am to you? Just some guy who works for your dad?" His voice was eerily quiet and deadly calm. "Close the door. We need to talk."

An entire brigade of alarm bells began to sound in my head. I knew Nico would not be happy about me avoiding him, but I hadn't expected him to be so upset. What had he expected? I'd made him no promises. He couldn't just waltz in after seven years away and expect that one night together would fix everything.

I tried to keep my growing agitation under wraps, knowing it wasn't going to help matters. Instead, I closed the door and told myself I'd listen to whatever he had to say before overreacting. "What do we need to talk about?" I asked as I folded my arms across my chest, mirroring his own stance.

"Aside from the obvious?" He lifted a brow to indicate the hot mess of our relationship. "We need to discuss a certain painting I saw at one of the bratva offices today."

Ideally, this was where I would have scrunched up my brow and feigned complete ignorance. However, his words were so unexpected, all I could do was struggle to keep my desperate panic from showing on my face. My heart rate doubled almost instantly, but I refused to let my breathing reflect its extra exertion. I kept my face impassive and my body totally motionless aside from perfectly controlled breathing. "I'm not well versed at Russian art but go ahead." The retort wasn't half bad, and I gave myself a mental high five. Not that it mattered. In every other respect, I was a deer sighted by the hungry wolf, and my chances were slim to none.

"I assume since the artwork was yours, you'd be very familiar with it."

"And what makes you think the piece was mine?"

"It was a painting of a pile of skulls. The same pile of skulls I watched you working on that night I came to talk to your father. The same skulls you were so worried about me seeing when I told you I'd watched you paint." His detached air heated with accusation as he laid the groundwork for his claims.

I shook my head and pulled out my phone. "Is this what you saw?" I thrust my phone forward, showing him an image of a painting. "It's called *Pyramid of Skulls* by Paul Cézanne. Yes, I was painting a lookalike, but people do that stuff all the time! It's like seeing a Monet or van Gogh knockoff at Bed, Bath and Beyond. I don't know why you'd think my painting would be with the Russians. Just because you've got an active imagination doesn't mean I've done anything wrong."

His eyes perused the image, then narrowed as I attempted to argue my way out of the conversation, but he never made a move for the phone. He eased off the wall and slowly stalked toward me, causing me to retreat backward.

"For the past seven years, it's been crucial for me to hone

my instincts and listen to my gut. You know what my gut is telling me right now?" he asked in a rumbling, seductive tone.

My back pressed against the opposite wall as I shook my head, unable to form a response.

"It's telling me you're full of shit."

My nostrils flared as I attempted not to act outraged. "I suppose it's your word against mine."

A wicked glint sparked in his eyes as the corner of his mouth quirked up. "Not exactly, Sofia, baby. If you don't want to tell me the truth the easy way, we'll just have to do it the hard way."

The hard way? What did he mean?

Nico would never hurt me.

At least, I didn't think he would. Suddenly, I wasn't so sure. "What are you talking about?"

Nico pressed his chest forward, caging me between him and the wall with his hands planted firmly on either side of me. "I'm talking about this beautiful body of yours." He eased in, placing sensual kisses down the column of my neck.

My head rolled to the side, unable to reject the delicious sensation of his touch. As his hands came up between us and massaged my breasts, a wanton moan escaped my lips. "*Nico...*" A breathless plea, but for more or to stop, I wasn't sure.

Suddenly, he lifted me, then turned to lay my back on the tile floor with his body stretched over mine. He kissed me long and hard until I was drunk on the taste of him, only breaking free of the fog when he lifted my shirt up over my head. He stretched my arms above me, wrapping my shirt around my wrists, then leaned in to kiss me again. When I made to pull my hands back down, I discovered he had used the strings on one of my aprons to secure my wrists together.

"What are you doing?"

"Shhhh, just trust me," he soothed, tugging at my wrists again.

I reluctantly allowed him to place my hands far above my head, only to realize he was tying them to the heavy wooden leg of my supply table.

Before I could argue, it was too late. My wrists were bound, and he was lowering to kiss my neck and chest. His hands tugged at my sweatpants, which gave easily, as they had only been held up by a loose drawstring.

"Nico, my parents! We can't do this in here," I whisper-yelled, starting to panic.

"Your parents went into the city until late tonight. No one's here but you and me." He sat back on his heels, admiring my prone form before him. "I should spank your ass for running from me."

My core practically dripped with moisture at his words. I'd never been interested in BDSM or kink, but something about Nico made everything sound good.

"My girl likes that, does she? I'll remember that. These nipples pebbled up so tight, they look like little pink candies I want to suck on all night long." His eyes lifted for a second before he rose to his feet.

A sliver of fear trickled down my spine. *He wouldn't leave me like this as punishment, would he?*

Before I went too far with that train of thought, he made a quick trip to my bookshelf and returned to my side. I had several strings hung in the room where I clipped inspiration photos. In his hand were some of the tiny clothespins I used to hang the pictures. He straddled my waist, and I watched in an intoxicating mix of trepidation and desire as he clipped one of the pins onto my nipple.

I gasped, arching at the intense sensation. It was fascinating—not entirely pleasure or pain, but a heady mix of both. He secured a second clip onto my other nipple, then tied a lose string between them. When he gave a gentle tug, it ignited sensation in both breasts at the same time. My mind felt like it might fracture. "Oh, *Jesus*, Nico ..."

"I told you this body was mine," he purred. "Never doubt that I know exactly how to use it." He pushed my knees back, opening me to him, then kissed a path from the inside of my knee to my core. I was already so aroused, and my sensitive flesh pulsed for his touch. When his tongue thrust inside me, then rounded up over my swollen clit at the same time as his hand tugged on the string, I thought I was going to pass out.

Over and over he worked me, building an inferno of desire in every cell of my being, but withholding the spark that would rocket me into flames.

"Nico, *please* ..." I sobbed, over sensitized and desperate for release.

"I need the truth, Sofia," he whispered against my core, his warm breath its own brand of torture.

"You can't do this. It isn't fair."

"You had a choice, Ladybug. You chose this." His tongue slowly lapped from my opening up my slit.

"I can't," I panted. "I can't tell you everything."

"Why not?"

"Because you'll make me stop."

"Who says?"

"Me."

"And if I promise not to?"

"You'll do it anyway."

"Then tell me what you can. You can trust me, Sofia." His fingers eased inside me and curved up, stimulating that perfect spot inside me.

"It was mine," I moaned the confession. "The painting's mine." I was unable to think straight or care about anything but finding my release.

He knew I had lied.

He knew it was my painting—so why fight it?

"And why was it with the bratva?" he pushed.

"I make forgeries, and they find buyers for me." There, I'd told him. The secret was out, and it felt amazing to free myself of the burden. "*Please*, Nico."

"That's my girl ..." His mouth covered my pussy just as his fingers pounded inside me, and his other hand yanked the clips off my tender nipples.

I screamed out my orgasm, erupting in a maelstrom of pleasure that radiated across my body. In that instant, I couldn't have cared if I'd given the devil my very soul. I was the embodiment of peace and light and everything good. But all good things must come to an end, and eventually, my consciousness slowly found its way back into my body.

Nico freed my hands, then sat next to me on the ground, lifting me into his lap to cradle me close. "Who are you working with in the bratva?"

I shook my head just a fraction. "I can't tell you that."

"Yes, you can. It has something to do with your friend Michael, doesn't it?"

As if he'd waved a smelling salt under my nose, I was instantly alert. Shooting out of Nico's lap, I grabbed my pants and began to dress. "What do you know about Michael?" I was clearly freaking out, but I couldn't help myself. If Nico knew about Michael, I was screwed. He would tell my father, and they'd both insist I stay away from him. That wasn't an option. Michael had become one of the best parts of my life, and I refused to give him up.

Nico stood and angled himself in front of the door, his features hardening. "What I know is the man doesn't exist. I couldn't find a goddamn thing on him, and that means he's not someone you should be hanging around."

"*Stop!*" I spat at him, shoving my finger in his chest. "You stop right there before you go any farther. Michael was the one who picked me up off the ground and brought me back to life after you left. So don't you *dare* tell me to stay away from him. If you didn't want him in my life, you never should have left." I squeezed past him, opening the door and thundering down the hall.

I went straight to my room and slammed the door. Nico could find his own damn way out, and he'd have one hell of a fight on his hands if he tried to follow me up here. I'd gone from blissed out to furious in two minutes flat.

He wanted answers, and he got them. What he wouldn't get was control over my life.

I wanted to be with Nico, but I wasn't willing to compromise certain things in the process. I didn't know where that left us, but the choice was up to him. I'd told him where I stood. He would have to decide if he would concede to my terms or if he was going to risk losing me for good.

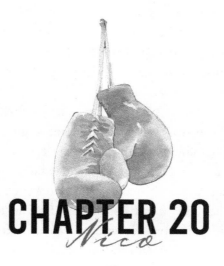

CHAPTER 20
Nico

NOW

What the hell just happened?

I stood alone in the quiet of Sofia's studio, her taste still on my tongue, wondering how the small progress we'd made had devolved so quickly. She had been pliant in my arms, finally confessing her sins to me when the mention of Michael made her more defensive than an injured animal.

For two days before I confronted her, I'd given her space while I came to grips with the fact that Sofia had changed as much as I had. I could have sought her out and demanded answers, but I decided to let things simmer. It also gave me time to look into her mystery classmate.

It had purely been morbid curiosity. I'd wanted to know who it was she'd befriended in my absence. When my searches for him turned up fake names and documents, it just created more questions. I hadn't had any proof that Michael was the connection between Sofia and the Russians, but there was no doubt after her reaction to the mention of his name.

The innocent black and red ladybug had morphed into a beautiful black widow.

Sofia had a darker side, and it was sexy as hell.

For all those years, I'd made sure not to go anywhere near her like a rehabilitated addict avoiding his drug of choice. I thought I was doing what was best. Her father protected her, so my presence wasn't necessary. Enzo kept her safe to an extent, but he didn't know her like I did. In my absence, she'd gotten herself into trouble without anyone knowing. They weren't able to see beneath the façade. After only a week back in her life, I'd ripped her secrets wide open.

She was endlessly tempting as my sweet, innocent Sofia. Discovering her darker side only made her siren's call louder. At this point in my life, being compatible with someone meek and innocent would have been a stretch. Knowing she could see me for the complex man I'd become and not run in fear made her that much more alluring.

Sofia had a little bit of devil in her angel eyes.

The problem was, her dark side was putting her in danger. The Russians were ruthless, and while we did business with them on occasion, we certainly weren't allies. I could hardly stop her from selling forgeries—who was I to judge her for her crimes?—but working with the Russians was out of the question. I could just as easily find her the contacts and help broker her deals without the added danger of the bratva.

Convincing her of that was going to be the hard part, and it didn't take a genius to know that now wasn't the time. I'd pushed her as far as she was willing to go for the night. Following her upstairs was only going to make things worse. We had plenty of time to work through our issues. Sofia slipped through my fingers once before, and I wasn't about to let it happen again.

CHAPTER 21
Sofia

NOW

"Everything's such a disaster," I told Michael once we were seated at the small breakfast place the next morning. "Nico and I were both keeping so many secrets; it's no wonder things went south. Now that he's back, everything's coming to light, and it's a hot mess."

"I always wondered why you didn't tell him about your family if you guys were so close. I would have asked, but you never wanted to talk about him." He looked at me sheepishly, as if I might get mad at him for admitting his thoughts.

"I get it—it doesn't make much sense. Nico was my happy place. It almost felt like I had two different lives—the school Sofia and the home Sofia. Put watercolor paints too close together, and they blur, becoming one. I didn't want the purity I had with Nico to be tainted by the uglier side of my family, so I kept it all a secret. Maybe it sounds odd now, but I compartmentalized from a very young age, so it's hard to explain."

"Actually, that does make sense. It was clear he meant a lot to you. You were even protective of his memory. I could see not wanting to mix the two."

"I'm sorry. I wasn't trying to be selfish by not talking about him. It just hurt so much." I glanced down at my mug of steaming coffee. "He was trying to protect me by leaving me, but he did it in a way that broke my heart. He hoped if he hurt me badly enough, I wouldn't bother fighting for him."

Michael's eyes narrowed, a malicious glint hardening his gaze. It gave me a rare glimpse of the danger others must have seen when they looked at him. "What do you mean, *hurt you badly enough?*"

"Not physically," I hurried to explain. "He broke things off in a way that would hurt, hoping I wouldn't ask questions.

"Sof, that doesn't make it better. I knew he left, but I didn't realize he'd been a dick about it."

"He had a good reason, I promise. I just didn't know that at the time." It surprised me to hear myself arguing on behalf of Nico. He had hurt me tremendously, but now that I understood why, it was hard not to forgive him. Deep down, I'd always wanted to find a way to forgive what he'd done. I'd loved him too much for too long not to.

"I'm not sure that absolves him in my book, but it's not my call to make." He paused momentarily as the waitress dropped off our orders. "So, why is everything a mess if he's come back and all is forgiven?"

His question brought back all the emotion of my argument with Nico, and my stomach balked at the sight of my food. "I'm not sure how it all happened, but he figured out I had a friend named Michael." I peered up at him through my lashes as I toyed with the hash browns on my plate. "Not only that, but he happened to see one of my paintings at a bratva office and managed to put it all together. He confronted me about it last night. Four years we've been a team, you and I, and not once has anyone in my family suspected a thing. In only a week's time, Nico tore off my mask and shook loose all my secrets."

"I take it that's a problem?" he asked, confused.

I licked my lips, unsure what to say. "Well, he apparently works for my dad now ... That was part of why he left."

His chewing slowed as he nodded. "I suppose a Lucciano man isn't going to want his woman to associate with the Russians."

It was my turn to be outraged, my gaze hardening. "It doesn't matter what he wants. I'll tell you now the same thing I told him last night. I'm not changing my life for him. Period. If he doesn't like what I do and who I do it with, that's his problem."

Michael smiled, but there was a sadness to it. "I appreciate you taking a stand, but I've always known this would be an issue someday. Our run lasted longer than I expected, actually."

"What the hell are you talking about?"

"Sof, between your feelings for Nico and our diverse ... *backgrounds*, we were as unlikely a pair as Romeo and Juliet—and look what happened to them." He smirked, unsuccessfully attempting to lighten the mood. This time, his voice softened, real emotion bleeding into his words. "It's why I never tried to take things further between us. It was obvious your heart could never truly be mine. Plus, we would never be free to have a life together."

I felt like the ground had opened and I was free-falling into a black hole where nothing made any sense. "You wanted me?" I whispered in shock. "You never said … I never knew."

He placed his hand over mine and leaned forward. "Sofia, how could I not? You're the most amazing woman I've ever known. It was just unfortunate for me I didn't get to you first." His crooked smile broke my heart straight down the middle, the tattered organ resembling a chewed-up dog toy rather than my heart.

Tears slipped from my eyes. I was the worst kind of fool. How had I not known?

"Hey," he called, drawing me back from my inner turmoil. "I'm responsible for myself. If being around you had been more than I could handle, I would have pulled away, okay? You didn't hurt me. Any disappointment I might have felt was my own damn fault. I've known from the beginning that I never stood a chance."

He was trying to make me feel better, but his words just made me want to rage at myself for being such an idiot. If I'd known, maybe I would have been able to let Michael fill the emptiness Nico had left inside me. Maybe everything would have been different. All the what-ifs surfacing in my life were dizzying. I felt horrible for Michael—for what I'd put him through—by not being able to give him that part of me. But since I'd already reconnected with Nico, there was no question what my heart wanted.

I had loved Nico since I was five years old.

He and I were two pieces of the same whole—no matter what had come between us.

I loved Michael, but my feelings for him simply didn't compare. I refused to give up his friendship, assuming he still wanted me around, but he would never be Nico. "I'm so sorry," was all I could muster past my tear-clogged throat.

"Don't be sorry. I'm not. You're my best friend and hopefully will be for a long time."

He squeezed my hand, drawing a small smile from me as the bell over the door to the restaurant jingled loudly. Two seconds later, our moment was interrupted by an enraged Nico towering over our booth.

"You need to take your fucking hand off her right now," he growled, glaring at Michael. His fists curled at his sides, making me recall his story about killing a man with his bare hands. The look in his eyes was murderous. There was no question he was still capable of such an act.

I leaped to my feet, inserting myself between the two men. "Nico, you need to calm down," I hissed, feeling the tension skyrocket in the small café.

"I'm not going to sit by and watch him hurt you. I don't know what kind of fucked-up thing is between you, but I could see whatever he said tore you apart, and I'm not okay with that. Get your stuff. We're leaving."

Michael eased from the booth, not remotely intimidated by Nico. "You're upset because you think *I* hurt her? Do you have any fucking idea how you destroyed her?" he bit out, his words a verbal lashing.

"Gentlemen, you need to take this outside before I call the cops," called out our waitress, interrupting the start of their pissing contest.

"Nico, Michael didn't hurt me. I was just upset. None of this is your business. You need to leave, *now*." I asserted as firmly as I could, desperate to prevent a fight between the two men in my life. "I promise we can discuss it later. I won't run. I know we need to talk, but this is not the time or place. *Please.*"

My words finally penetrating, Nico's eyes released their hold on Michael and dropped to where I stood with my hands pressed against his chest. His face was wrought with indecision, but when he glanced at the waitress holding her cell phone in her hand, he released a frustrated breath.

"Tonight you're staying with me—no more running—and we're working this shit out." His eyes demanded my compliance, which I readily gave.

"Okay." I nodded quickly. "I'll be there, I promise. Now, please, let us finish breakfast before she calls the cops."

Nico shot one last icy glare at Michael before retreating to the door. The second he was gone, I took a deep, steadying breath, and the hum of conversations picked up around us.

"He's intense, that one," Michael said humorlessly as he slid back into the booth.

"He wasn't always," I replied sadly. "The years have changed him, but it happens to all of us."

Michael paused with his fork midair, tilting his head. "You're still every bit as in love with him, aren't you?"

His observation stunned me.

I started to respond twice before I managed to make any sound. "Yeah, I think I am."

He nodded with a small smile. "Then you need to give him a shot—a real one. No grudges or resentment. You need to be open with him and let him in."

The truth of his statement resounded in a place deep in my chest. He was right. I owed it to us both to give us a second chance. To finally explore the potential of what existed between us. "I will, I promise."

He speared a sausage link, then winked. "Good, now eat. I'm gonna have to leave one hell of a tip, and I want my money's worth."

Shaking my head, I dove into my food with a grin.

CHAPTER 22
Sofia

NOW

'll pick you up from work. The text came in from Nico just after lunch, stirring a swarm of radioactive butterflies in my stomach. Excitement, anxiety, fear—nearly every emotion on the spectrum fought for dominance inside me.

Gallery closes at seven. I offered in response.

I know. Of course, he did. I should have expected nothing less.

That left me with just shy of five hours to kill before we had our come-to-Jesus talk. Never in all my life had five hours lasted so long. Despite every distraction technique I tried, the minutes ticked by agonizingly slowly. Teetering on a precipice for the better part of a day was exhausting. By the time six rolled around, I was ready to get our talk over with one way or the other.

Nico was waiting for me outside when I exited the gallery.

I drew on every shred of courage and fortitude I had and walked to his car. Without a word, he opened the passenger door for me, helping me inside. Seconds later, he slid into the driver's seat and pulled away from the curb, all in total silence.

I wasn't sure what I'd expected, but it hadn't been this.

My nerves already frazzled, the quiet was more than I could bear. "So, where do you live now?" I blurted, hoping to ease the tension.

"Not too far," he said, never taking his eyes from the road. Clearly, Nico had no desire to start any semblance of a conversation in the car.

Uncomfortable silence it is.

He pulled up at a skyscraper in Lower Manhattan right on the water's edge. A doorman helped me out of the car, then took the keys from Nico and left with the car after a quick greeting.

"Fancy," I murmured, taking it all in.

He placed his hand on my lower back, directing me forward. "It has a shit ton of amenities, which means I don't have to go anywhere if I don't want to."

The lobby was beautifully designed—the term casual elegance came to mind. There was a fireplace along one wall with enormous shelves above it. Together with an assortment of seating and tables, the setup resembled a traditional living room but for dozens of people instead of just a few.

Nico led me to an elevator where we rose to the thirtieth floor, which housed three apartments. His home was absolutely stunning. Floor-to-ceiling glass walls were the focal point of the space, overlooking an almost too-perfect view of the city. His décor was all neutral—soft tans and grays—allowing the skyline to steal the show. The sun was setting, painting the sky in warm reds and yellows. It was the perfect backdrop for the twinkling city lights starting to pop across the landscape. I was so taken by the sight that I hadn't realized I'd been staring until Nico's voice brought me back to the present.

"The amenities are great, but the view is what sold me," he said quietly beside me.

When I glanced over at him, his eyes were fixed on me rather than the breathtaking view. I dropped my gaze, my cheeks heating at his implied compliment. "So, how is this supposed to work?" I ventured warily. "I'm not sure what to say or how to do this."

"First, I'd say we're probably both hungry. How about we eat, then talk?"

"What do you have? I can help cook, if you'd like."

"I have a grocery service, so I'm not sure. We'll have to dig around and see what's there." He paused, then grew more serious. "I don't have an answer for any of this either, Sofia, but I know we won't get anywhere unless we talk. That's all tonight is—a chance for us to catch up and figure out what we want from one another."

A little choked up, I simply nodded and followed him to the kitchen area. When had my Nico grown so mature? He was always observant and introspective, but after seeing bouts of his temper, I hadn't realized just how levelheaded he still was.

We gathered the fixings for some simple pasta with meat sauce and a salad. Nico cooked the ground beef while I washed vegetables, all with relaxing music playing in the background. Every now and then, my gaze would collide with his or we'd both reach for something at the same time, and the innocent flirtation brought me back to our high school days—the times when the charge between us was building, promising to create something beautiful.

The food was ready too quickly, putting an end to the simplicity of the moment. We made our plates and sat at his dining table, Nico taking the head of the table so as to sit next to me rather than across.

I moaned with my first bite, savoring the delicious spices. "This is amazing. How did you learn to cook so well?"

"It's my mom's recipe. When she moved out, I spent a lot of time with her at her new place. She taught me all my favorites, and I made sure she didn't go back to my dad."

"What made her finally decide to leave?" His father was an ass, but she'd been with him for so long, I'd doubted she would ever leave.

"She figured out I wasn't going to school, so I told her what had happened. I told her everything. She spent the next month getting ready and never looked back. I worried she might waver. It wasn't easy going out on her own after so long, but she was a trooper. Now, she wishes she'd walked away years earlier."

I nodded, taking a sip of the wine he'd brought out with our plates. "Change is hard. Even when it's good change, it can still be scary."

My eyes flitted to his briefly before dropping back to my food. We spent the next few minutes eating together in silence. It wasn't totally comfortable, but less tense than our time in the car. Eventually, we both set our forks down, and Nico rose, reaching out for my hand.

"Let's leave the dishes, they can wait."

I didn't argue. Allowing him to help me from my seat, I

placed my hand in his and followed him to the living area where he gestured for me to have a seat on the couch with him. My legs naturally angled in toward him, and he turned his body toward mine, resting his arm over the back of the sofa.

"Sofia, you can't keep running from me. This thing between us is still very much alive. I know you feel it too."

Before arriving, I had promised myself I'd give him the truth, no matter how terrifying. "I do feel it," I confided softly. "And I want you to know that I forgive you for what happened. Now that I know your reasons, I understand why you did what you did. We were both at fault—too many secrets coming between us."

Nico's gaze grew more intense as he scooted even closer to me, our legs touching. "And I hope you know that I don't give a fuck if you want to paint forgeries. Actually, I think it's sexy as hell." His fingers trailed down my arm, then came back up to lift the chain around my neck and reveal the Eiffel Tower pendant. "You can't imagine how happy it makes me that you still wear it."

"It's the best gift I've ever received. Even when you broke my heart, I never took it off."

"You're too good for me, Ladybug. Don't get me wrong, I'm keeping you anyway, but no matter how many laws you break, you'll always be perfect in my eyes."

I wanted to dive into his arms, but I held back, knowing we still had an important issue to work through. "What about Michael?" I asked hesitantly.

Nico's eyes darkened, his lips thinning almost imperceptibly. "Is he the only obstacle between us? Is there anything else I need to know?"

I shook my head. "He's the last of my secrets."

He gave a determined nod. "Then we'll figure it out. I'm not about to let him come between us."

I started to ask for clarification, unclear what he meant, but he placed a finger over my lips.

"Sofia Genovese, I've loved you every minute of my life since I was six years old. I've thought about you endlessly and dreamed about you each night. I promise you, we will figure it out together. Okay?"

I nodded with his finger still pressed to my lips, my heart a melted puddle of goo at my feet. I loved this man so much it was incomprehensible. Just being there with him, my wounded soul felt patched and whole.

Nico's callused fingers reached behind my neck and pulled me gently forward, bringing my lips to his. Our previous kisses had a combatant, feisty nature to them but not this one. This kiss was pure love and forgiveness. Without taking his lips from mine, Nico lifted me in his arms and carried me to his bedroom.

"I've fucked you and toyed with you, but now I want to make love to you. You'll see. We'll get this all sorted, and then I'm going to make you my wife so that you and everyone on this fucking planet knows you're mine." He leaned in again, this time kissing me with all the pent-up passion that simmered between us.

I couldn't have argued if I'd wanted to. Not that I did.

It was all I'd ever wanted my entire life.

We both stripped bare, no clothes or secrets between us, and made love under the dim glow of the city lights. Our love making wasn't leisurely or gentle because that wasn't the nature of our love. Nothing about Nico and I was casual or delicate. We were intense and passionate—our intimacy lasting long hours until we were both utterly spent. And even then, we remained tangled in each other's bodies, unwilling to part.

I chose to trust that he spoke the truth about Michael. Assuming that was the only obstacle we had to surmount, I saw no reason we couldn't finally have the life together that we'd always dreamed about.

This time, I had no trouble drifting off into a dreamless sleep with Nico's body pressed tightly to mine. Sometime in the deep hours of night, I woke alone when a haunting piano melody drifted into the room. Nico's side of the bed was cold, and I wondered how long he'd been up. Grabbing his button-down shirt, I slipped my arms in it and padded in search of the music. Around the corner and down the hall, a door was cracked open, and beautiful music flowed from within.

I pressed the door open farther and leaned against the frame, watching Nico play a gorgeous grand piano in the dark, clothed only in his boxer briefs. The sinewy muscles of his back flexed and flowed as his adept fingers danced across the keys. The song he played was moving—not altogether sad, but heavy with longing and need. It made my heart swell to see him playing when he'd been so passionate about it as a boy.

Slowly, the tune came to an end, and Nico turned toward me. "Come here," he ordered in a raspy voice.

When I was close enough, he pulled me between him and the keys, staying seated and gently pulling apart the shirt to expose me to him.

"I thought you said you didn't play much anymore."

"I may have fibbed. I did stop for a while, but when I got

this place, I soundproofed this room and started playing again." He absently traced a line down between my breasts and to my navel.

"Why would you fib about something like that?"

He peered up at me, his cobalt eyes fathomless. "I think I wanted you to know that I didn't just carry on without you. I hated myself for what I did. That's why I quit. I didn't deserve the peace and beauty I got from playing. Not after what I did to you."

"No more guilt, though, right?" I trailed my fingers along his stubble-lined jaw, the tickle stirring a warmth in my belly.

He leaned in, kissing his way down my stomach, then pressed my backside onto the keys, making a cacophony of sound. Lifting my feet onto his bench, he spread my knees wide between him and dove in to play his other favorite instrument.

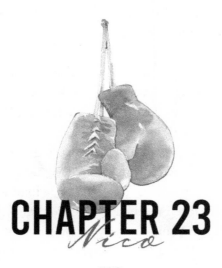

CHAPTER 23
Nico

NOW

I would have liked Sofia to stay naked in my bed all day, but she insisted on going to work. After fucking her senseless in my shower, I drove her to the gallery and went in to check on my own business matters. Not only did I have work to do, but I also needed to figure out how to get Sofia untangled from the Russians and quietly. She'd never want her parents to know, so that made things tricky.

Seeing her with Michael made my skin crawl with the need to break up their little breakfast date and pound him into the ground. I forced myself to stay put for what seemed like ages, watching them chat like it was the most natural thing in the world. It was important for me to see their dynamic before I could work on cutting him out of her life.

Every bit of patience I had expired when she began to cry. I couldn't take it any longer. I didn't know what the hell he'd said, but it was over. I was back in Sofia's life, and there wasn't room for another man in her world.

Especially a Russian.

I said we'd work it out, and I meant it, but I doubted my version of working it out would be her ideal scenario. The situation was delicate and would take finesse. Not exactly my forte, but I'd figure it out.

The morning passed quickly, making me forget about lunch until almost two. I ran to a nearby deli to grab a sandwich, and on my way back to the office, a loud whistle caught my attention before I reached for the front door. It could have been anyone whistling for any reason, but it snagged my attention like a fishing hook had yanked me straight from the stream.

Pausing, I scanned my surroundings and zeroed in on Michael almost immediately. He stood on the opposite side of the street with his hands tucked inside his jacket pockets as if he were a simple pedestrian out for a stroll. When my eyes landed on him, he lifted his chin at me, then made his way over. Every muscle in my body coiled in anticipation of a fight —it was a sensation my body knew well. If he planned to challenge me, he was going to regret it.

"Have a minute?" He wasn't giving off any confrontational vibes, but I wasn't letting my guard down.

"Let's take a walk," I offered in the cool tone of indifference, concealing the rage stirring inside me.

"I know I'm the last person you want to talk to, but I think it's important we do this and not make Sofia act as a go-between," Michael started conversationally. "You need to know that she and I are good friends, but it's never gone past that. Don't get me wrong, I would have if I could have, but there was never enough room in her heart for the both of us. That was clear from day one. The reason you need to understand that is because I know you'll want me out of her life, but the only thing that's going to do is hurt her."

"And keep her safe," I added smugly.

"Would you say she's endangered by your mafia associations?"

"Not from *my* family."

"Exactly. You and me, we're no different. I care about Sofia too, and I'd never let anyone hurt her either. I want her to be happy. I'm not just arguing for my own benefit. If you try to come between us, you'll break her heart without achieving any positive result. You've already hurt her unnecessarily once; don't do it again." His voice took on a hard edge, adding an extra threat to his warning.

I glared at him, hating the fucker for rubbing it in my face but unable to argue. "What am I supposed to do? Let her continue to do business with the bratva and not tell her father?"

"Let me talk to her about handing over the business aspects to you, if you're willing to do that. If Sofia and I keep our relationship purely based on friendship, would that be agreeable to you?"

Agreeable was hardly the word I would choose—tolerable would fit better, or maybe sufferable. "I'm sure you make a nice little profit off her work. You'd be willing to give that up?"

"It was never about the money for either of us. As long as she's happy, that's all that matters."

Fuck. He was being totally reasonable, and I knew it. But it was also clear he was one hundred percent in love with her.

How was I supposed to let her spend time with another man who had feelings for her? On the other hand, how could I in good conscience deny her access to her best friend? I was fucked either way. "I don't like it, but I'm not sure I have any options."

"Welcome to the club, man." Michael looked at me, and for a moment, he dropped his playboy easygoing front, allowing me to see the pain he carried. It was only the briefest glance, but it was enough. He'd been stuck playing second fiddle to me for the past seven years. I was glad he'd been there for her but couldn't imagine why he'd stuck around. It had to have been torture being near her all that time and knowing he could never have her.

"It's fucked up. You not moving on." I couldn't help from commenting even though it was none of my business.

"You're telling me," he muttered. "My eyes aren't closed to other options."

"Good, because I don't want to spend the rest of my life worrying about this. Until you find someone else, you keep your dick in your pants when you're around Sofia."

"Right, I'll try to remember that," he shot back sarcastically. "Listen, there's one other thing I wanted to tell you. A week ago, a guy approached Sofia outside her dorm asking questions about me. He claimed to be a cop, but my sources didn't turn up anything. Called himself Detective James Breechner—the name mean anything to you?"

Just when I started feeling like the threat level was down, a completely unknown variable is brought to my attention. "Never heard the name before. What did he want?"

"She didn't give him the chance to ask questions after he asked about her relationship with me. He hasn't shown back up or contacted her again. I wanted you to know so you could keep an eye out."

The last thing I wanted was to like Michael, but he made it hard not to. I should have given Sofia more credit not to buddy up to an asshole. I wanted to hate the guy for obvious reasons, but that was looking less and less possible. We weren't going on any fishing trips together or shit like that, but I was willing to admit he might not be all bad.

My phone began to buzz in my pocket, the display telling me Enzo was calling. "Let me grab this ... Yeah."

The gravity in Enzo's voice had me instantly on alert. "I just got a call. Sofia's in danger."

CHAPTER 24
Sofia

NOW

I hadn't stopped smiling all morning. It was amazing what love and several mind-blowing orgasms could do for a girl's outlook. I wasn't a moody person, but I also wasn't typically chipper either—no one had ever volunteered me for the Miss Congeniality ballot.

Nico had dropped me off at work with a packed lunch and strict instructions not to leave the gallery until he picked me up at the end of the day. He admitted that he'd been following me since being assigned guard duty and spent most of his days in his car watching me. Though I was a little disappointed in my observational skills, I was glad to know I'd had a protective eye watching over me. We decided if I wasn't leaving the gallery, he could spend the day at his office and get caught up on some of his own work.

When I got a text from Michael asking me to meet him at a coffee shop two doors down from the gallery, I knew I'd be safe with him, and it was only about thirty feet from work. What could happen in thirty feet? Plus, it was broad daylight in busy Manhattan. I was worried there'd been a development with the cop and wanted to hear what he had to say.

It was midmorning, so only a couple of people were at the counter, neither of whom were Michael. The place had a small seating section in the back, so I scooted past the line to check back there. The moment I rounded the corner, something heavy crashed down on my head and everything went dark.

HADN'T WINTER ALREADY ENDED? Why is it so cold? I thought it was spring, but everything feels so fuzzy.

My mind stirred to life in a groggy haze of confusion, cold, and pain—most noticeable was the pounding headache that pulsed angrily at the back of my head. As my eyes fluttered open, I wondered if I'd passed out after drinking and was hung over. None of it made sense.

I went to rub my aching temples and found that my hands were bound by a series of zip ties, as were my ankles. Adrenaline shocked my brain back to functional capacity, making me recall my search in the coffee shop and the pain that brought on the darkness. I bolted upright to sit on the frozen concrete floor and discovered I wasn't alone.

"Finally, you're awake. I started to think maybe I'd been a little overzealous when I hit you." Sal. My father's former best friend paced the small room in a wrinkled suit with several days' worth of stubble on his jaw. I'd never seen him anything less than impeccably dressed. The sight of him so disheveled and frenzied was enough on its own to unsettle me. But knowing what had happened to Alessia and waking with my hands and feet bound left me absolutely terrified.

"They've been watching you so carefully," he continued, resuming his pacing. "Alessia's jumped in bed with that fucking Russo cunt, and Maria wasn't an option, so you were my best bet, but I was starting to get worried I'd never get you alone. It was a lucky thing your father forgot to revoke my access to his phone account. I just had to log in to get your cell records—a little software to jumble the signal, and I was able to lure you to the coffee shop with a simple text. With a car in the back alley, getting you here was almost too easy." He gave me a maniacal grin as he finished.

He'd completely jumped off the deep end. Had he always been this way and simply hidden it? What did he want with me? "Why are you doing this?" My voice shook from fear and the cold. I didn't want to sound so pathetic, but I didn't feel capable of much else.

"Because your father's got half the East Coast after me, the fuckin' moron. If it wasn't for the fact that I have to hide inside, I'd be laughing my ass off knowing I'm right under his nose still on Staten Island. You're my leverage to get out of here with my heart still beating. That reminds me ... the phone, I need the phone," he muttered, patting his pockets. "I'm gonna call Enzo, and I know him—he'll demand to talk to you. That's why I had to wait for you to wake up. You tell him you're fine, but you better not say one damn thing more. I need you alive for now, but that doesn't mean I need you in one piece—got it?" He glared at me with gray, soulless eyes, then pulled open a thick, sealed door and vanished.

My dad—I was going to get to talk to my dad. Relief and

hope made my eyes sting with tears, and my lungs shuddered with the start of sobs, but I quickly pulled myself together. I had to find a way to tell my dad where I was, but how? What could I say to tip him off that I was still on Staten Island without Sal understanding?

Still on Staten Island.

My necklace.

I reached up and lifted the pendant, but before I could work on the clasp, the door began to open. I yanked as hard as I could, ripping the chain from my neck and tucking it in one of my jean pockets.

Sal entered my frozen cell, eyes glued to a disposable phone.

"Uncle Sal, it's so cold in here. Please, can I have a blanket or something?" This time, I was more than happy to infuse my voice with weakness. I had a plan, and I wanted Sal to see me as totally helpless so he wouldn't get suspicious.

"It's hardly on refrigerate, so you'll be fine. If your father does what he's supposed to, you'll be out of here soon enough." He never looked at me, muttering his response as he fiddled with the phone and some other device he was holding.

Looking up, I realized there were evenly spaced rows of sliders along the ceiling as if used to hang stuff throughout the room. *Was I in a walk-in freezer?* Why had the asshole put me in a freezer? Was giving me a concussion and tying me up not enough? I had been the goddamn flower girl at his wedding, and now he couldn't have cared less if I was bleeding out before him.

This man was a total sociopath, and I'd had no idea. I considered myself exceptionally observant, but he'd fooled even me. Panic made my muscles begin to seize and clench even more than they already were fighting off the cold. I was wracked with full-body tremors. He didn't think it was too cold, but he had a hundred pounds on me and was in a full suit. I had a thin blouse and jeggings on—my teeth were chattering so bad my jaw was already aching.

"Enzo, it's been a while ... Yeah, save the threats for someone who cares. I have little Sofia here, so I need you to listen up ... That's better. You call off all the hunting dogs— you, the Russos and Gallos, and especially the fucking Russians. I want safe passage from the city, and once I'm out, I'll tell you where you can find Sofia ... I figured you'd ask— here." He placed his hand over the receiver and glared at me with challenge, showing me how much he'd enjoy punishing me for any misstep.

I attempted to take the phone in my hand, but he swatted my hands away, holding the phone to my ear. "D-d-dad?" I shivered, unable to help my chattering.

"Sofia, are you okay?" His voice was wrought with concern, making my chest constrict with the desire to run into the safety of his arms.

"Yes-s-s-s, but I l-l-lost my n-n-necklace, I'm s-s-so s-s-sorry."

Sal yanked the phone away from me, narrowing his eyes as he studied the angry red mark on my neck. I could imagine he was wondering if it had been there before and whether it had been pulled off when he transported me or if I was trying to pull a stunt.

"That's enough," he spat into the phone. "Your daughter is a little cold right now. You're going to want to follow my instructions or this could go very badly for her. I'll send you instructions on where to find her, but only once I'm safely out of the country. You lay a hand on me until then, and she's dead." He ended the call, his eyes gleaming with victory. Without another glance at me, he left the freezer, slamming the door behind him.

Until he left the country? How long would that take?

I wasn't sure how I'd manage an hour, let alone a full day or more.

Unable to lean against the cold wall, I curled into a seated ball, my arms hugging my legs to my chest as best as I could without the zip ties cutting off circulation to my hands. The room was eerily silent once my frantic thoughts finally calmed. Maybe it was good that I couldn't hear a compressor pumping in more cold air, but it was hard to see any bright side to my situation. If watching a pot until water boiled slowed time, sitting trapped in a meat locker made it positively endless. It was just me and each of my frozen breaths puffing out in little white clouds.

Okay, Sofia, not helping.

I shook myself mentally and struggled to my feet before hopping over to the door to verify the lunatic had indeed locked me in. The heavy metal wouldn't budge. Though it had been a long shot, it was worth checking. Trying not to be discouraged, I reminded myself to keep moving. My dad would find me, and I needed to be alive when he did.

I hopped for a bit, but the zip ties began to cut painfully into my ankles, so I resorted to closed-leg squats and yoga sun salutations. I alternated sessions, doing fifty of one exercise, then resting for a bit. When my teeth began to chatter again, I'd get up and do fifty of the other movement.

Over and over.

For what had to be hours.

Sal never came back, and the room never got any warmer.

It was impossible not to let the shred of hope I'd been cultivating slip through my frozen fingers. Fear was insidious —like a cockroach, it was impossible to kill and thrived in the worst conditions. The what-ifs played endlessly on shuffle in my head, a twisted soundtrack of questions and doubt.

The stabbing pangs of hunger were the final straw. I hadn't cried since I'd been there—I'd teared up, but never allowed myself to fully let go. After doing hundreds, if not thousands, of exercises and sitting through yet another round of painful shivering just to add hunger to the mix, I finally broke.

I lay my head down on my arms, legs pulled to my chin, and I sobbed.

I cried until my ribs ached and my throat burned from the heaving sobs. As the tears began to dry on my numb cheeks, a bone-deep exhaustion crept over me like I'd pulled an all-nighter studying or taken a slug of cough syrup. It was probably a bad idea to sit still for long, but I was so incredibly tired.

If I just rest my eyes for a few minutes, maybe the time will pass faster. Maybe by the time I wake up, Daddy will be here to rescue me.

It was just too tempting. The discomfort and fear were such a drain, and the promise of sleep's oblivion too enticing to ignore.

Just a few minutes...

They say fate was fickle, but time was just as unpredictable. What seemed like a few minutes could be hours, and what was supposed to be days might feel like minutes. I had no idea how long I dozed, but it had been long enough. When I roused from sleep, I felt excruciating stiffness in all my joints, frozen in place while my muscles trembled uncontrollably.

I needed to get up and move—to get my blood pumping through my body—but I couldn't even get to my feet. Repeatedly I tried, only to lose my balance or have my body cave under the pressure.

How long had it been? Would my dad come through that door any minute, or was my rescue still hours away?

I'd never make it.

I was so cold, and I couldn't imagine I'd ever be warm again. More tears threatened, but I was too tired for sobbing. All I could do was lay on my side, my hair the only barrier between me and the frosty concrete. My top shoulder rocked me, just an inch or so of motion, back and forth. It was soothing, like being in someone's arms.

Nico's arms.

I'd only just got him back. Would I ever get to feel those strong arms wrapped around me again?

All those years, the only place I could see him was in my dreams. I became proficient at designing and manipulating my dreams to keep Nico in my life. I had known it wasn't healthy, but I didn't care. It was the only way I could have him, so I took what I could get. If sleep would give me a reprieve from the misery of my situation, then that was what I would do.

I closed my eyes and escaped into my dreams.

CHAPTER 25
Nico

NOW

"What do you mean she's in danger?" I shot back at Enzo. Terror narrowed my focus to the sound of his voice, everything else fading into oblivion.

"Sal has her. I'm not sure what shape she's in, but she could hardly talk she was shivering so badly. I don't think we have long. He's demanding we allow him to leave the country—says he'll give us her location once he's free. I'm gathering as many guys as we can to start looking for her in the meantime." His tension was audible in the tight strain of his voice.

"You talked to her?"

"Only briefly. She mentioned losing her necklace, but I have no idea what she meant. I'm not sure if she was out of it or trying to tell me something—that mean anything to you?"

Her necklace—Paris. Sal wanted out of the country, so she wasn't in Paris. When I'd given her the necklace, she'd told me she would be happy staying on Staten Island as long as we were together. "She's on Staten Island."

His deep exhale made a whooshing sound across the line. "Okay, that's good. It'll help narrow the search. We already had guys watching his house, so we know he's not there. I don't know where he's hiding, but we'll find him."

"Let me know if you hear anything else."

"I'll check back with you shortly." The line went dead, and I stared at my phone in desperation. How the hell were we supposed to find her in a city of millions? "You hear the conversation?" I asked Michael.

"Yeah, you have any inkling where he might be hiding?"

"I can't imagine he'd be holed up anywhere near our people."

"Where else would he be on the island? You Italians practically run the place."

What he said was true. Staten Island was predominantly populated with Italians—not necessarily mafia related, but Italians, nonetheless. We bred like rabbits. It was hard to run into someone who didn't know you in a roundabout fashion.

Think, think, think.

Enzo said she didn't have long. I need to figure out where she is and do it fast.

"He said she was shivering so bad she couldn't talk," I mused, thinking out loud. "So maybe she's being kept in a fridge or freezer."

"What, like at a grocer or a butcher?"

"Something like that, but who knows where." I searched the street helplessly, frustration and despair attempting to put a stranglehold on me. "*Fuck,*" I hissed, trying to keep from crushing my phone in my clenched fist.

"Grocers tend to be larger operations—more employees and complications. My money is on a butcher. I say unless we have a better plan, we just start checking butchers. We can start on the north end of the Island and work our way south."

"Works for me," I muttered. "I have nothing better to suggest, and I don't want to just sit on my ass doing nothing."

"Let's go. I'll drive." He turned and sped down the sidewalk, making me jog to catch up.

We drove from Manhattan through Jersey, then started at Ranchers Best Meat not far from the Bayonne Bridge. When that was a bust, we hit the Elm Park and Tompkinsville butchers without any luck.

"Google shows one in West Brighton, so we can hit that next. Head toward the zoo," I instructed without taking my eyes from Google maps.

"That one's closed."

"Maybe that's the perfect place to check then."

"I can't imagine Sal would have dared use the shop. It was bratva owned, located in the largest Russian community in all of Staten Island," Michael explained.

We were both quiet for a moment. Then our eyes met at the same time, and I could see his thoughts had taken him to the same place as mine. It was possibly the one place on the island that the Italians wouldn't dare look for Sal, which made it the perfect hideout—so long as the Russians didn't figure it out.

"I assume you have my back on this," I noted. "In any other circumstance, I'd need to set something up with Biba before I could go snooping on Russian property."

"You're with me, so there's no problem. And I wouldn't

turn my back on you. It would be the same as turning my back on Sofia. Not gonna happen."

Michael tested the limits of his car, weaving in and out of traffic. While he drove, I let Enzo know what we'd been up to. He hadn't heard anything from Sal, and in this case, no news was *not* good news. We parked two doors down from the butcher shop and decided I'd take the front while Michael went around back. I waited out front while Michael used his lock-picking skills to get in. I tried not to get my hopes up, knowing how slim our chances were. I figured at least the venture kept me occupied and allowed me to feel like I was doing *something* to help.

After a minute or so, the front door opened, and Michael ushered me inside, a gun already in hand. As soon as I was off the street, I followed suit and took out my weapon. Aside from the meat having been removed, the place looked otherwise untouched.

"There's a stairwell by the back door to what I assume is an apartment upstairs," Michael whispered as we made our way behind the front counter.

When we soundlessly passed through the swinging door into the prep room, we both turned to one another. The air inside was noticeably warmer from the air compressor, and there was rope wrapped between the freezer handle and a pipe parallel to the door. I rushed to the door, untying the rope and pulling it open while Michael covered my back.

A gust of cool air met me, along with the sight of tiny Sofia, curled into a ball on the floor. I rushed to where she lay, my heart in my throat at the sight of her blue lips and ghostly white skin. "Sof, wake up!" I rubbed her cool arms, cursing and pleading for her to show me signs of life. I forced myself to remain still just long enough to watch her and see the small movement at the pulse point on her neck.

She was alive.

Thank Christ.

"Is she alive?" hissed Michael, edging in from the door.

"Stay outside that door. I don't want us all trapped in here. She's breathing, but we gotta get her warmed up." The air wasn't actually as cold as I'd feared, but her prolonged exposure to it had her core temperature dangerously low. I carefully lifted her in my arms, but before I could take a step, a sound came from somewhere inside the shop.

My eyes met Michael's, and a silent communication passed between us—I would keep Sofia safe; he would handle whatever was up front. I carried her out of the freezer but stayed in the prep room while Michael quietly snuck out to the front counter.

Seconds later, gunfire rang out in the small shop—a series of rapid shots shattering the quiet around us. I dropped to a squat, holding Sofia tight to my chest, my back turned to the entry. The exchange only lasted a matter of seconds, then the room fell back into silence.

"*Fuck!*" Michael barked in an angry yell. "You can come out, Nico. He's gone."

I rose to my feet, then peeked out the front, doing my best to keep my gun out while still holding Sofia. Michael was leaned against the side wall, hunched over, and blood was spreading out from a gunshot wound in his thigh.

"I can't believe I fucking let him get away," he bit out, slamming his fist against the wall. "Must have been the stairs creaking that we heard. I caught him just as he came around the corner, but I didn't expect him to be armed. We both shot, and he took off. I got him in the shoulder but couldn't chase after him."

"We can't worry about that now. Sofia needs to get warm, and you need a doctor. Can you get to the car, or should I call an ambulance?"

"Let's get her home first. I'll be fine once I tie it off." He pulled off his belt, then cinched it around his upper thigh.

"Lean on my shoulder." I opened the front door, holding it open as the two of us fumbled our way outside. Once he was in the back seat, I set Sofia in his arms, then drove like a bat out of hell toward Enzo's place. I gave him a heads-up we were on our way, and he put a call in for the family doctor to meet us at the house. If at all possible, we avoided going to a hospital. They kept records and asked questions, and we weren't a fan of either of those things. While Sofia could be treated at home, Michael's injury would likely involve surgery, and thus, a trip to the hospital.

When we arrived at the house, one of our guys was waiting and ready to get Michael the medical attention he needed. I gave his hand a firm shake, assuring him I'd send updates about Sofia. He wasn't crazy about leaving, but I told him he'd only hurt her if he bled to death rescuing her. He called me some choice names but begrudgingly agreed to go.

As soon as we were inside, I asked Enzo if we could use his master bathtub. Carlotta led me to the bathroom where she helped me start a bath and undress Sofia. As we removed her clothes, she began to shiver, tremors shaking her entire body.

"Take care of my baby," Carlotta choked out, her face lined with worry.

"She'll be fine as soon as we get her warmed up, and the best way to do that is in the bath. Water conducts heat far better than air," I said, my words meant to reassure me just as much as her.

She nodded, then quietly let herself out of the room. I quickly undressed and carried Sofia into the warm bath. The water felt almost cool to me, but we didn't want it too warm so that it hurt her already traumatized body. As I eased us into the water, she let out a small whimper. My heart soared at hearing her show any sign of life, even if it sounded pained. I positioned her back against my front, laid her head back on my chest, and held her close.

Seeing her so weak and fragile, I would have given anything to help her, my life included. Ending things between us had nearly killed me, but at least I'd known she was alive and well. I wasn't sure how I would survive if I lost her for good.

"Come on, Ladybug. Come back to me," I crooned in her ear. "I just got you back; don't leave me now."

For a half hour, I worked on warming her body. I would let out some of the water, then add back in warmer water to reheat the bath. Slowly, her tremors eased as her seizing muscles warmed and relaxed, but she never woke. Eventually, I lifted her from the water, slipping on the robes Carlotta had left for us, then carried her up to her bedroom.

Her mother had used an electric blanket to warm her bed, so when I removed Sofia's robe and placed her beneath the sheets, she curled up peacefully and slept. I was going to sweat to death, but I didn't care. I wasn't ready to leave her. I crawled in beside her, wrapping my body around hers in a cocoon of warmth.

CHAPTER 26
Sofia

NOW

I woke from a muddled dream when I tried to roll over and was met with a sharp stinging in my hand. A peek through squinted eyes told me I had an IV in my hand. Why did I have an IV?

"Easy, Sofia," Nico said from behind me. He had been propped against the headboard while I slept and was now scouring my face, but I wasn't sure for what.

I pulled myself up to a sitting position, making my entire body ache. The sensation brought back the memories of lying cold on the freezer floor, feeling like I'd never be warm again. At the recollection, my entire body shuddered.

"It's okay, Ladybug. You're home now." He pulled me over to gently kiss my temple.

"Oh, Sofia! Enzo! Sofia's awake!" my mother called from the doorway. Hand to her chest, she hurried to my bedside as tears pooled in her eyes. She sat beside me and cautiously wrapped her arms around me, careful not to tug on the IV tube. "My sweet Sofia, you had me so worried."

I held my mom as tight as I could without straining my aching muscles and gave a tight smile to my dad as he entered my bedroom. "Hey, Daddy."

He stepped close and placed a kiss on the top of my head. "Hey, Princess. It's good to see you awake."

Nico started to stand, but I took his hand and held him securely in place. "How long was I out?"

"Fourteen hours since Nico brought you home."

"Nico?" I turned to him in surprise. "How did you find me?" I sputtered, curious at everything I'd missed.

My mom stood, patting my hand. "You guys talk. I'm going to put on some soup for you." She left the room, and my dad took her place on the edge of the bed.

"Nico figured out your clue about being on Staten Island," my dad explained. "The rest was a little bit of luck and persistence. He had the help of a Russian man who I'm told is a friend of yours." He arched a brow at me. "Apparently, we have a lot to talk about when you're feeling better."

There was only one Russian Nico possibly could have been working with. I didn't know how they did it, but the two had gotten together and rescued me—just in time, if my aching body was any judge. I was glad to be alive, but it meant my father now knew my deepest secret.

I took a deep breath, my body sagging as I exhaled on a nod.

"Sof, there's something you should know," Nico said, bringing my attention back to him. "Michael's okay, but he was shot while we were rescuing you."

My head whipped back to Nico, terror hurtling my stomach into my throat. "Shot? Where? What happened? Is he okay?"

Nico held up his hand to calm me down. "He's going to be fine, but he had a gunshot wound to the leg that needed surgery. He insisted on getting you here to start warming you up rather than letting me call him an ambulance. He's a hard-headed bastard."

I was so relieved he was all right, but my heart hurt to know he had been shot. "That sounds like him. He's always been super protective of me."

"You'll definitely have to tell us all about it," my dad interrupted. "I can't believe my little Sofia was buddied up to the bratva without me having a clue." He smirked and shook his head.

If one good thing had come from all of this, it was having my Italian family be more relieved I was alive than upset about my Russian friendship. Had I told them a week ago, before any of this had happened, I was sure my father would have been livid. The sight of him laughing about Michael gave me hope that my father might allow the relationship to continue.

I smiled back at my dad. "It just kind of happened. It wasn't exactly something I sought out."

"How about you tell me the whole story tomorrow? For now, let's get you some of Mom's soup and let you rest. You were hypothermic and had a nasty concussion. The doctor checked you out and said you were fine to recover at home, but I'm sure he'll want to know you're awake. I'll see if Mom needs help and give the doc a call. And Sofia, go easy on this guy." He gestured to Nico. "I'm not sure he slept at all last night." Dad kissed my head again, giving a small nod to Nico before leaving.

When I peered back at Nico, I realized he had dark circles under his eyes and his hair was a wavy mess. "Thank you for saving me and for staying with me last night."

He pulled me against his chest, lowering us to the bed. "I've never been so fucking terrified in my whole life. Hearing you were missing was bad, but then seeing you lifeless and blue on the floor ... worst moment of my life." His voice was a soft rumble, even deeper with my ear over his heart. His hand stroked my hair, then traced a line around my neck.

"I had to tear off my necklace so I could give Dad the clue without Sal knowing."

"We'll get it fixed. Even better, let's just go to Paris."

A smile crept across my face. "That sounds nice, but I'd really like my necklace."

Nico grunted. "We'll do both then."

I giggled, snuggling closer, then grew somber as my thoughts regressed to my ordeal. "I love you, Nico," I confessed softly. "I've loved you for as long as I can remember. When I was trapped in that freezer, all I could think about was that I'd never see you again, and that scared me more than the thought of dying. I know we may still have stuff to work out, but you're it for me. Always have been, always will be."

His fingers tilted my chin, bringing my face to his before his lips brushed mine in a tender kiss. "You're everything to me, Ladybug. I know a lot of things went wrong for us, but sometimes, that's what has to happen before things can be right—before we could arrive at this very moment."

"I think so too," I whispered.

"Love you, Ladybug."

"Love you too, Nico."

CHAPTER 27
Sofia

NOW

"This shit ends *now*," I insisted.

If I hadn't been so caught up in what I planned to say, I would have laughed at the stunned expressions on my family's faces. First thing the next day, I'd called my parents and sisters together, along with Nico, for a sit-down. My opening line seemed to grab everyone's attention.

"No more secrets, no more lies. Our lives are complicated enough; the last thing we need is to keep secrets from one another. Not only that, but it weakens us. If we can't rely on each other in this life, then we have no one. I don't want that for myself or any of you. I should have said something a long time ago, but I got caught up in the lies and my own issues." I turned to my parents, softening my tone. What I was going to say would tear them apart, but I needed to come clean. "If I'm going to lead the charge and air all my dirty laundry, then I have to go back to the beginning. Daddy, that night Marco was killed, I wasn't asleep. I saw the whole thing."

My father's eyes, usually so guarded and stoic, suddenly became a window to the crippling pain he carried inside him. I recognized it instantly because it mirrored my own. We bore the same ugly scars that night had marked us with, and for once, we could share in our heartbreak with someone who truly understood. I leapt from my seat and flung myself into my father's welcoming embrace.

"Baby girl, why didn't you tell us?" My mom's voice shook as tears filled her eyes.

I pulled back from my father, but he didn't let me go. Instead, he made room beside him on the sofa and held me snugly against his side. "I'm not really sure," I tried to explain. "I was terrified and confused. I couldn't understand why Dad left Marco bleeding on the ground or how he knew how to fight. I knew I wasn't supposed to see what had happened. When he got back in the car, I closed my eyes and hid, pretending to be asleep. I think I just shut down, unable to face what had happened. Then, when you all told the story of how Marco had died, I knew it was a lie but couldn't understand why. It took me a while, but I watched and learned. Once I figured out about our mafia ties, it made it easier to spot all the other lies."

My mom shook her head, heartbroken she'd had no idea what I'd been going through.

Alessia's mouth gaped open, stunned that I wasn't the perfect angel she always teased me about being. "You knew the whole time? I just learned about the family from Luca. I had no idea."

"Luca?" I asked, eyes darting to my father.

"He's a member of the Russo family," my dad explained.

My head tipped back in a slow nod. "That explains a lot, but I still want to know exactly what happened with Alessia—the *truth*."

"*I* want to hear just how the Russians entered the picture," Dad said pointedly.

I gave a guilty smile. "Alright, my story first, but I want to hear hers too."

For the next half hour, I told them about my secret life—about the paintings and Michael. Nico volunteered to unveil what had happened to him and the story of how he'd pushed me away. We took turns, giving explanations and opening up to one another—Nico and I, along with Alessia and my parents.

The process made me feel more connected to my family and loved than I ever had before. There was vulnerability in sharing your secrets, but there was also a tremendous reward. I was trusting them with my truth and was honored when they did the same. The process knitted us together, bonding us in a way simply being related hadn't.

The only person who was notably silent was Maria. My father admitted that Maria had been a part of the outfit for many years, but Maria offered no further insights into herself. I couldn't force her to see the benefit of sharing, but I hoped one day she would. It was a tremendous relief to unload those burdens, and I highly doubted she was simply burden-free.

Once we finished our discussion, we enjoyed lunch together, conversation flowing much more naturally than it had at our past family dinners. It was amazing how at ease everyone could be when we weren't watching every word and attempting to put on a front. I loved my family, and I wanted nothing more than for us to be a close-knit group. Could we maintain the open channels of communication I had initiated?

Only time would tell.

After lunch, Nico took me to the hospital to visit Michael. Seeing the two men together in one room was odd. They represented two vastly different phases of my life—like Scrooge witnessing the ghost of Christmases past, I was unsettled and on edge. Fortunately, Nico was totally at ease, helping to calm me. When we walked in, he went straight to Michael, offering a firm handshake in greeting. I wasn't sure what all had gone on between the two men in my absence, but their exchange was a far cry from the near brawl at the diner.

"Hey there, handsome, how you feeling?" I asked, giving him a hug and ignoring Nico's huff behind me.

"A whole lot better now that I see you're alive and well. You scared the shit outta me."

"Ditto. It wasn't exactly fun to wake up and hear you'd been shot."

"I'm fine. He didn't hit an artery or anything. Now that they patched me up, I'm good to break out of here."

"Michael Garin," I scolded, finger to his chest. "Don't you dare think of leaving one minute before those doctors discharge you."

"One brush with death, and suddenly, she's all about following the rules," he teased with a smirk.

"I don't know about that, but I do know this wouldn't have happened if you weren't trying to save me. I don't want you getting an infection or not healing properly because of me."

His brows came together as his eyes hardened. "You listen to me, Sofia. This was not your fault, so I want you to wipe

244 | JILL RAMSOWER

that shit from your mind. The only one who gets the blame is Sal Amato, you got that?"

My lips thinned, and I nodded, but the guilt tugging at my heart didn't simply wash away. It was hard to know that someone I loved had been hurt trying to help me. It was even worse knowing that person had been hurting for years because he'd wanted more from me than I could give.

"Something else you guys should know," added Michael. "A friend came this morning to let me know they took care of Breechner—found him snooping around the gallery. He was some schmuck private investigator hired to look into a forgery. The guy who bought your first reproduction was trying to sell it off to someone else, and that guy had his insurance company assess the painting. The appraiser pegged it as a forgery, so the deal fell through. Our buyer got his panties in a twist and decided he'd come after the seller. Both Breechner and his client have been made aware of their error and won't be a problem any longer."

"I appreciate your family helping with that." I was surprised that I didn't feel the fear and regret typically associated with being caught. Instead, it just made me want to work harder until my artwork was indistinguishable from the originals.

"I was impressed the guy was able to trace the painting back to me," Michael mused. "We go through enough middlemen to make that a difficult feat. You were just at the wrong place at the wrong time. Regardless, it's probably best we're transferring things to Nico and the Italians—change things up and keep the waters murky."

My head snapped up, surprise widening my eyes. "What? What do you mean transferring things to Nico?"

"Nico and I talked things over and decided it would be best if you ran your operation through his outfit. You and I can still be friends, but we'll remove the business from our equation. It keeps things simpler, and you still get to do what you do best. That work for you?" Michael asked with a hint of humor in his voice.

"Uh … yeah, I just … you guys talked it out?" When did that happen? I was stunned. Why hadn't Nico told me on the way over?

"We were actually in the middle of talking when your dad called to tell Nico you were in trouble."

I glanced back at Nico, whose face was impassive as he listened, leaning against the far wall. I gave him a soft smile, sending him all my gratitude and love.

"How are we feeling, Mr. Garin?" a nurse asked as she entered the room.

"Ahhh, time for my medicine. That's the only bad thing about this place. They're stingy on the meds."

I wrapped my arms around Michael, hugging him tightly. "I'm going to let you rest, but you text me later."

"Will do. Another twenty-four hours, and I should be out of here, so no more worrying."

We said our goodbyes and I left feeling significantly better than when I arrived. Nico had said Michael was fine, but I had to see it for myself to ease my worry. An hour later, we were back in the city at Nico's apartment. The second he walked us through the door, he had me up against the wall with his mouth on mine.

"I've been patient, letting you recover and visit with friends and family, but I'm done waiting. I need you naked." The tender, affectionate lover was gone, and the possessive,

246 | JILL RAMSOWER

demanding Nico was back. He raked his teeth along my neck, thrusting his hard length against my belly.

His need drove me crazy, making me just as hungry for him as he was me. I pulled his T-shirt up over his head, then fumbled with the button on his jeans. I dropped to my knees, pulling his pants down with me, then slowly dragged my hands up his muscular legs to grip his hard length. That was when I saw the tattoo just inside his left hip bone. It was small enough that I hadn't noticed it before, but at eye level, there was no missing it. There were two Chinese symbols, and above them was the word "love" and below, "Ladybug." My right hand released him to gently touch the word.

"You were always with me, a permanent part of my soul. It only made sense my body should reflect that."

I leaned in and kissed the inked dedication to our love, then peered up at him as I took his entire length into my mouth. Nico's chest flared out as he took in a ragged breath. I showered him with all the love and devotion I was feeling until he demanded I stop and lifted me into his arms, impaling me against the wall.

"Fuck, Sofia, you feel so good, so tight," he breathed harshly.

My hands rested on his shoulders, feeling the coiled muscles flex beneath my fingertips. "More, Nico. I need more," I moaned, wanting him to brand me—make me his forever.

Nico did not disappoint.

He pounded into me until my body couldn't take any more. He didn't just draw an orgasm from me, his body commanded it, and mine was helpless but to obey. My legs and core flexed and quivered as white-hot pleasure exploded inside me, coursing through my veins. At the same time, Nico pumped his release inside me, continuing with gentle thrusts to ride out every last ounce of my orgasm.

For a moment, we leaned against the wall, recovering with shaky breaths. Then he gingerly carried me to the bathroom and set me on the counter before wetting a towel and cleaning me.

"I feel like I'm getting the royal treatment. Is this the normal protocol?" I teased, not expecting the dark look that hardened his features.

Nico tossed the washcloth into the sink and lifted me back into his arms. "I wasn't exactly a saint while we were apart, but I want you to know that I never touched another girl before that night at the party. I know I said there were others, but there weren't. I had to get drunk off my ass before I could stand to let Brooke touch me. I've never made love to anyone until you, and there will never be anyone after." He lowered me into his bed, his hard body over mine.

"Okay," I whispered.

"Good, now I want to fuck you slow and sweet before we go grab some dinner."

"Again?"

"We have a shit ton of missed time to make up for, so I'm going to be inside you a lot." His eyes darkened, and his lips pulled up in the corners.

"What about my stuff? I work tomorrow and need to get my things."

"You're moving in with me. I'll have your stuff brought over from your parents' house."

"Moving in?" I gawked. "Nico, we just got back together."

"For seven years, I've missed out on that smile of yours, so

I'm not wasting one more minute apart. You need time to decide if you want me?"

I shook my head, knowing he was the only man I'd ever want.

"Then it's decided. We'll cancel your lease, pay whatever default we have to, and get your shit moved in here. If we need more space, I'll see about buying one of the places next door, and we can join the two units. As long as you're here with me, everything else is just a technicality."

"Okay," I whispered again, too shocked to say anything else.

"If this conversation is over," he rumbled before rolling his tongue around one of my nipples. "I'd like to fuck you now."

"Okay."

With the one simple word, he was inside me—mind, body, and soul.

EPILOGUE
Sofia

Nico wasn't kidding when he said he'd take me to Paris. It had taken a number of heated discussions because I had to quit my job in order to go, but eventually, he wore me down. He argued that I'd be traveling too frequently to hold a job, and I liked the idea too much to argue for long. I enjoyed working at the gallery, but it had only served a purpose for the old Sofia. Now that my secrets were out, there was little purpose for a day job.

Two weeks later, we were on a plane about to have the ten most magical days of my life. The cherry on top was how excited I was to come home to my family. My plea about becoming closer had struck a chord, and everyone made an effort to be more open.

The jury was still out on how I felt about the extended family, but we would see soon enough. Despite a killer case of jet lag, the day after we got home, Nico and I had a multifamily Fourth of July barbecue to attend. It wasn't just a gathering of distant branches of the family tree—my father explained that this was the first Five Families joint party since before my brother was killed and a war had broken out among the families.

"Are you ready?" I called from the front door. "We're going to be late!"

Nico came around the corner, an eyebrow raised at me in challenge. "In a hurry, are we?" He was so damn edible, I could have drooled. His snug T-shirt and khaki shorts with flip-flops gave him an almost preppy look, but his partial sleeve tattoo peeking from beneath his shirt said there was more to the man.

"You know I'm excited. Now, quit making me wait."

"But I have a surprise for you. It came while we were away."

I hadn't noticed he carried something curled in his large fist. Opening his hand, a pool of silver chain lay on his palm, the Eiffel Tower charm in the middle.

"You had it fixed?" I had no idea he'd taken it to a jeweler. I'd been too busy with the trip to mess with it myself.

He lifted the chain and worked the clasp. "I told you I'd give you both—Paris *and* your necklace. I'm a man of my word."

Once he put the necklace on me, I turned around and threw my arms around his neck. "Thank you, baby. I love you so much."

"Love you, Ladybug."

I lifted my legs around his waist and pressed my core against him.

"I thought you said we were in a hurry," he murmured against my lips.

I nipped at his bottom lip and smiled. "Five minutes won't kill anybody."

An hour later, I texted Alessia to let her know we'd finally arrived—better late than never. We weaved our way through the enormous crowd as I steered us over to where Alessia and Luca were seated by a gorgeous pool.

"Sofia!" she squealed as soon as she spotted us. "How was the trip? It's so good to see you." She engulfed me in a warm hug.

"It was absolutely amazing, and … well … this happened." I lifted my left hand to show her the stunning engagement ring Nico had given me at the Eiffel Tower. It was somewhat cliché, but for us, the monument had so much meaning that it was perfect.

"Oh my God! Luca, look! Sof got engaged! Oh, Sofia, it's gorgeous." My big sister was appropriately mushy, oohing and aahing over my ring and our engagement story. Luca gave Nico a bro handshake-hug combination as they talked between themselves.

"We haven't heard much since we were out of the country. Any news on Sal?" I asked Alessia, keeping my voice down.

"Not that I've heard. We figure he found a way out of the country, but they're still looking."

Just thinking about the man made me want to hit something. "I figured if he'd been found, someone would have gotten word to us. Just wanted to double-check. I'm not letting that piece of shit ruin our day. Tell me what else I've missed while we were away."

Just as she opened her mouth, a loud thumping sounded

over a microphone. "Excuse me, everyone," a deep, masculine voice said.

We turned to look for the source and found a heavily tattooed man standing by the house along with my father and several others.

"I want to welcome you to my home," the man said, and everyone began to clap.

"That's Matteo De Luca," Alessia whispered to me. "He's the one who rescued me from that monster who hurt me. He's the underboss of the Gallo family."

The Gallos. They were the ones who had been behind my brother's death. My father stood next to Matteo as though all had been forgiven, but I wasn't sure I felt the same. I'd lived my whole life thinking of them as the enemy.

"It's been many years since we've had a gathering of this size," he continued. "And it's our hope that it will become a tradition again. We are all stronger united in friendship than when we are at each other's throats. All of us should do our part to help align ourselves in this new movement toward harmony. It is in that vein that I would like to announce my engagement to the stunning Maria Genovese." He held out his hand, and to my utter astonishment, Maria stepped forward and placed her hand in his as the crowd erupted in cheers.

My jaw hanging open, I turned to Alessia, who looked just as shocked. We gaped at one another, unable to say a word.

"Thank you, thank you. We hope to ring in a new era of prosperity and peace among us all. Please, enjoy the party and thank you again for coming." Matteo waved to the crowd with a broad smile, but I didn't miss how Maria slipped her hand from his the moment his speech was over.

This was going to be interesting.

Thank you so much for reading NEVER TRUTH!
The Five Families is a series of interconnected standalones,
and the next book in the lineup is Blood Always.

Blood Always (The Five Families #3)
It should have been a simple arranged marriage, but fate had
other plans. He saw her untamed independence as a challenge.
She saw his alluring authority as a threat. Their lives were
altered irrevocably—from enemies allied by a strategic
marriage to something dark and consuming.
Something that tasted like obsession.

Want more of Michael?
In the novelette Guilty Stars, Michael gets the delicious
happily ever after he so deserves. Don't miss it!

Didn't catch the beginning of the series?
Check out book 1, Forever Lies, to learn about Alessia and the
chance elevator encounter that changed her life forever.

A NOTE FROM JILL

Sofia and Nico came to life for me as I was writing this story. My heart bled for them as their heartbreaking journey unfolded, and I hope you were able to experience the same joy and grief over their tumultuous relationship and traumatic pasts.

I'd like to offer a sincere thank you for purchasing *Never Truth*. If you enjoyed reading the book as much as I enjoyed writing it, please take a moment to leave a review. Leaving a review is the easiest way to say ***Thank You*** to an author. Reviews do not need to be long or involved, just a sentence or two that tells people what you liked about the book in order to help readers know why they might like it too.

ACKNOWLEDGEMENTS

This time around, I have two groups I want to thank. First, a heartfelt thank you to my reader supporters who have gone above and beyond the call of duty. Kaitlyn, Kristi, Leah, Sonya, and Elizabeth are at the top of that list. You didn't know me from Adam but jumped on my bandwagon and have been invaluable helping me spread the word about my books (and some of you even help me craft the stories themselves). Your encouragement, friendship, and support have been priceless to me!

Secondly, I want to offer my humble gratitude to a number of crazy generous authors who have taken me under their wing and helped guide me through my author infancy. Amelia Hutchins held my hand when I was utterly clueless and has been there with answers to every banal question I could send her. Jennifer Bene, aside from being delightfully hilarious and unerringly sweet, imparted a wealth of next-level information to help me get my books in the hands of readers. Cora Reilly, Ashleigh Zavarelli, and Natasha Knight welcomed me into the world of mafia romance when I decided to branch out from my urban fantasy roots. I feel incredibly blessed to work with you ladies. Thank you for your time, knowledge, kindness, patience, and most of all, your friendship.

ABOUT THE AUTHOR

Jill Ramsower is a life-long Texan—born in Houston, raised in Austin, and currently residing in West Texas. She attended Baylor University and subsequently Baylor Law School to obtain her BA and JD degrees. She spent the next fourteen years practicing law and raising her three children until one fateful day, she strayed from the well-trod path she had been walking and sat down to write a book. An addict with a pen, she set to writing like a woman possessed and discovered that telling stories is her passion in life.

SOCIAL MEDIA & WEBSITE

Release Day Alerts, Sneak Peak, and Newsletter
To be the first to know about upcoming releases, please join
Jill's Newsletter. You can find the signup on my website!

Official Website: www.jillramsower.com
Jill's Facebook Page: www.facebook.com/jillramsowerauthor
Reader Group: Jill's Ravenous Readers
Follow Jill on Instagram: @jillramsowerauthor
Follow Jill on Twitter: @JRamsower